Hired Gun in Hell

It is 1858 and the new Texas is expanding, moving closer to the *Comancheria*, Indian Territory. Around the little settlement of Bantillo, precariously placed east of San Antonio, the bullets and the arrows fly. The land is teeming with Comancheros, and sometimes the Comanche from up north raid over the Red River.

A stage has been chartered, and the travellers inside all have their own stories. Leon Brett and Watt Duggan want to assemble a new community – the Liberocracy, living off the land and water by the shores of the Kimishi River – while Sir Thomas Rowan, speaker and writer, has a message of civilization. Then there is Miss Emily Nolan, actress and singer, out for her first trip West; politician Harvey Caldy and his dream of railroads; and finally there is the real celebrity: tall Joe Jardine, infamous gunman known as the Leveller – a man who puts right what the law has failed to do.

But Jardine meets an old enemy – the man who killed the woman he revered – his wife. He's a hired gun in hell, and he has to get even with the killer he has hated, while saving the rest of the party from more danger.

Hired Gun in Hell

Frank Callan

A Black Horse Western

ROBERT HALE

© Frank Callan 2019
First published in Great Britain 2019

ISBN 978-0-7198-3033-4

The Crowood Press
The Stable Block
Crowood Lane
Ramsbury
Marlborough
Wiltshire SN8 2HR

www.bhwesterns.com

Robert Hale is an imprint
of The Crowood Press

Typeset by
Derek Doyle & Associates, Shaw Heath
Printed and bound in Great Britain by
4Bind Ltd, Stevenage, SG1 2XT

CHAPTER 1

The stage rumbled on, out into the wilds of the borderlands. Fear wrapped around it like a stifling blanket. Every canyon was a place where some murderous crew might be assembled, ready to ride out, screaming and yelling, to take the horses, the people and the stage itself, because everything out in this hellish nowhere was threatening – even the silence.

On top, at the reins, was Snowy Macree, aged but not giving in to life yet, and with him, riding shotgun, was Ben Scott, twenty-two and too dreamy for his own survival, most said, back in Marshal, Harrison County, where the stage was bound.

'I knew this was a crazy idea . . . I mean, who chartered this old heap of rotten wood, to go out here where a man might get killed?' Scott asked the older man.

'Well, the bookish folk in Marshal did . . . and they got other bookish folk in Bantillo, see? They wanted to make sure that their guest speaker got to their places safe, like. Should have hired more than one man, though – should have got themselves a troop of soldiers.' Snowy screwed up his face and added, 'But I been on this route a few times . . . generally fine. But I wish I was back up in Galveston staring at the sea.'

It was late summer, and the war with Mexico had ended ten years earlier; but there was a considerable slice of unease, and Snowy was keen to maintain the nervy atmosphere. Everyone had been talking recently of the rogues, outlaws and drifters working along the Red River from Lamar to Grayson, and that was too close for comfort.

'You keep them eyeballs fixed on the horizon, Mister Scott. You hear? I been almost a corpse and embalmed by the damned bandits in these parts. Back in thirty-five it was. Thought I was fated to be burned and skinned. They was a bunch of Tonkawas and Mexies, with a slack-ass captain who ran away from every woman he seduced, and washed up livin' as a madman let loose on the staked plains.'

'I am watching, Mister Snowy, I am watching. Anything moves, any little prairie dog or rattler, and I'll put a bullet in it, sure as my daddy is a whiskey-head!'

'Well, you keep them eyeballs keen and sharp, right? I'm very fond of my scalp . . . still got white hair and two ears!' Snowy slowed down the pace, and inside, the passengers were glad of it.

The most talkative of the folk in the stage was a distinguished-looking man of around fifty-five, with a full grey-black beard and moustache, rich black hair and a ruddy face; he was slim, and dressed in a smart suit of reserved black, with a showy, fancy vest beneath. This was Sir Thomas Rowan, English aristocrat, knighted by the Queen herself, a man full of so many words that they rushed out, all wanting to be heard at once.

'I have to tell you, that ridiculous speed we have experienced was absolutely unnecessary. I shall be reporting this to the Chairman of the Lecture Circuit when we reach San Antonio, you may be sure of that. Here I am, a man of advanced years and delicate constitution, subjected to the bone-shaking indignity of this supposed carriage . . . it's actually a device for torture, as used in the Spanish Inquisition.'

'Oh, there's no harm done, Sir Thomas. You have a very strong set of limbs there . . . and I'm speaking as a medical man.'

'Yes, Brett, I'm sure you know the facts. But then you are not inside my skin, are you, dear fellow?'

Leon Brett, thirty-five, was a Londoner, fresh from his medical studies at Guy's Hospital, and so full of dreams that he let reality slip away at times. His friend, Watt Duggan, looked like what he was, a farm labourer. He was from Norfolk, and had met Leon when he was his patient, suffering from the cholera, and the doctor had saved his life.

'Where on earth are you young gentlemen going anyway? I'm signed on to give a lecture in Bantillo and then in Marshal . . . but you two, well I mean, you seem far too delicate to survive out here, for God's sake!'

7

'My dear Sir Thomas,' Leon Brett answered, with a smile, 'Don't underestimate the resilience of an apothecary! When you have undertaken surgery with a saw and knife, you fear very little . . . I've been a dresser to the very best surgeons in England. I've stitched arteries and sliced off limbs. . . .'

'Oh . . . oh my Lord!' There was a squeak from the only woman present in the stage, and she almost fainted at hearing those words. The only other occupant was a big, rangy man with long fair hair and a fondness for leather, as his body was swathed in dark, worn leather from collar to breeches. She recovered herself, though Jardine had moved across to help if needed. 'Hell, Doc, you scared the girl worse than a finger o' lightnin' on the range spooks the steers! Watch your tongue around the ladies, please. . . .'

'It's quite all right. . . .' Brett looked at the girl, and he saw that she was fine; she was made of tough material, he thought. The big man grunted his satisfaction that everything was OK. He sat back again, and tilted his hat over his face, trying to sleep.

'Miss Nolan, please accept my deepest apologies,' Leon Brett said, offering her a sip of brandy. She revived and managed to assure him that all was well. Things returned to normal, and Sir Thomas pressed the young Englishmen about their purpose in going to so barren a part of the new continent.

'Leon is a man with vision, Sir,' Watt Duggan cut in, 'He and I are going to put a footprint in this wonderful land, a footprint of freedom. It is to be called a Liberocracy.'

Brett was a little embarrassed at this. He did not really want his aims to be known as yet. But now all heads turned to look at him. Even the tall man tipped up his hat and stared.

'Well, now that it's been mentioned I have to explain, I suppose. You see, a short while ago, as I was reading a periodical, I learned about a notion conceived by the poets Southey and Coleridge, to start a new community out here in America . . . it was to be called a *Pantisocracy*. Mr Coleridge wrote much about it. The community was to be a new, hopeful beginning, to point humanity in the proper direction . . . people living together in harmony, with discord unknown and each person's abilities and disposition fulfilled and nourished.'

The tall man laughed now. He sat forward. 'Don't tell me fella, it was ravaged by the Indians and every individual was killed . . . sorry ma'am.'

'No, in fact they never came over the ocean. They were defeated by the planning difficulties. Er . . . what is your name again, Sir?'

The tall man said, 'Joe Jardine, mister. I live by my gun. Fact is, I'm here to take care of you folks, good paid work, and even better, you can't run away. I got you all in here, where I can see you. '

'Oh, I see. A gunfighter.' Brett said, his tone suggesting a criticism.

'I don't like that word, my friend . . . prefer to be known as a professional put-righter. I'm a Texan, and I don't back down if a wrong has been done.' He liked the reaction, when they all looked at each other, confused. He changed the subject. 'This pan-tiwhatsit . . . I bet you my last dime that the women was to run it . . . was to cook, was to make the shirts and was to be no more'n slaves! That's the way of this world, mister doctor.'

'Yes, Mr Brett, the man has a point. I am trying to escape the fate of being a slavish housewife by doing what my mother and father did – tread the boards!' Emily Nolan said.

'You are an actress?' Sir Thomas asked, and when the affirmative answer came back, his face showed his low opinion of the young woman.

'I am also a singer. I play the piano as well, and I have comic monologues in my repertoire. Emily Nolan . . . that's my name.'

'You will one day find fame, I'll wager!' Watt Duggan was smitten with her, and it showed.

The quiet man, Harvey Caldy, who had told them all about his railroad promotion business, said he loved a woman who could sing. 'It's a room in paradise, a lady singing!' he said. 'When the first railroad steams down this way, heading for Mexico, I'll have a real smart entertainment carriage, and you will be my entertainer, Miss Nolan!' He thought about lighting a cigar but then recalled that he had been politely asked to refrain from doing so.

'I am intrigued by this Liberocracy, young man, tell me more, do!' Sir Thomas said, with a wry smile on his face, promising a degree of ridicule. But Brett went on, regardless:

'Look, I appeal to everyone here to consider what

a parlous state the world is in! Look around, read the papers, attend meetings, and what will all this tell you? It will depict a world in confusion! Yes, 'tis so. Men have lost their way.' Brett was warming to his subject now. 'Even the best of us, the politicians and philosophers . . . they are lost! Why, everywhere the classes are at war, and the nations too! I am a medical man, and so I have seen the worst that one human may do to another. Before I left Liverpool to come to this world of future happiness, I witnessed the most terrible sufferings and deaths, inflicted on one person by another . . . the great lords of industry . . . they build and build . . . engines and locomotives . . . but the poor labouring man is pressed down to dwell in a cellar amid disease and agony. His children starve. He riots in the streets! I tell you, that will not happen here . . . in this new world a true Liberocracy may be constructed . . . it is a land of open minds, free thinking and without the restraint and fear instilled in the working man back in the tired old world . . . '

'Good . . . very good, so therefore, young buck, what would your Liberocracy do about this crowd of heathens . . . out there, see!' Joe Jardine nodded through the side window, and passengers' heads turned. They all saw a bunch of men on horses riding towards the stage.

Up top, Snowy was lashing the horses, and Scott was trying to aim his rifle at the leading rider. 'Who are they, Scott? They gonna skin us or guard us?' Snowy shouted, above the din of the stage's rattling

11

and swaying as it picked up speed.

'I think they're maybe friendly. I can't shoot yet.'

A bullet slammed into the wood by Scott's leg and he snapped out, 'Hell, no, they ain't friendly, Snowy! Comancheros I guess. A rag-bag. I can see feathers and caps, and I can see skin on some and cloth on others ... yep, Comancheros. I'm gonna shoot at 'em ... git ridin' quick as you can ... we could make that arroyo ... see, to the right.'

Snowy thought there was maybe five hundred yards between the stage and the end of the arroyo. They could dart in beside some cottonwoods and scramble to some rocks. Scott fired again. His new Colt Dragoon gave him quick repeated fire. His Ranger friend Jack Makin had given it to him, to save his neck in a tight fix, as he put it. This was a tight fix.

'Well, I reckon there's fifteen of 'em ... and they fancy some plunder!' Joe Jardine said. 'You got weapons, you men?' He looked around. Sir Thomas brought out a revolver and nodded. Brett took out a bag and extracted his longest surgeon's knife. Watt had the oldest handgun that Jardine had ever seen. Quietly, he prayed to the Almighty for help, because boy, they needed it.

Scott swivelled around now, facing the nearest rider. He managed to take aim and send a bullet into the man's chest. The rider went down in an instant, and Scott hit out at the air with a whoop of joy.

Snowy carried on raising the whip and cracking it down on the horses' backs. They pounded the dry earth: nearer and nearer came the end of the little

12

rocks by the arroyo. Then a rider with a bow and arrow came up by the side of the stage. He was a Tonkawa, but wearing a white hat and a military coat. He shot an arrow which stuck into the fabric of the stage next to the window, and then, riding closer, he lunged at the board by the door and took his dagger, to slash at the nearest face. But Jardine's pistol put a bullet in the man's cheek before he could do anything, and he fell away with a scream.

The stage reached the safety of the nearest rocks, and Snowy pulled it around so that the side faced the oncoming riders. 'Everybody out and on the ground!' Scott shouted. They scrambled around to cower below the window height, with Scott and Snowy now both with rifles aimed at the attackers, one at each end of the stage. Jardine ran to a rock about ten feet high and found himself a spot where he could see everything. He had snatched his rifle from his pouch on the stage floor.

The riders came at them, screaming to try to instil some fear. Arrows and bullets lodged in the stage, and some hit the earth. Jardine had easy prey though: his first shots brought down three men, who all went to their deaths with a rap of their heads on hard rock. The others pulled up, dismounted, and crouched behind the animals, to fire from safety. Their losses were heavy and their victims were in a strong position. Bullets came at them, killing their mounts now.

Harvey Caldy had two revolvers and he blazed away at any shape moving at them. He then scuttled

13

behind rocks for cover, trying to escape the worst of the close combat that inevitably followed. But, as he discovered after feeling a shattering of bone in his arm, he was hit, and he lay in agony, in some little shadow he found.

Someone from the Comancheros screamed out some words in Spanish, and there was a rush, as they all took to a run and went for the stage. Jardine's shots rang out and more men fell. But two attackers reached the stage. One put an axe in Scott's head and another swung a rifle butt at Snowy, just as the old man shot his assailant through the eye.

The Englishmen were left to wrestle their enemies, as Emily ran for deeper cover. Watt more than held his own. His strong frame gave him the solidity of a rock, and he battered the first man who came at him, then took the next in a neck-hold, twisting him so much that he screamed for mercy.

Brett had a heavy man lunge at him, and then, when his fist had missed any contact, the man was on Brett, trying to choke him. He was so close that the stink of him filled Brett's nostrils. The sweat from him was greasy. The will to live filled every inch of Brett's body, and he took the long knife he held and raised it upwards, part of it scraping his belly, before he found enough space to stick the blade deep into the man's neck. Blood gushed out, drenching them both. The attacker was pushed off, and rolled into the dust to die.

One attacker saw Emily and made straight for her, raising an axe, which was meant to split her head open. He was a half-breed Mexican-Comanche and he could move fast, but Joe Jardine was quicker. He saw the man charge, took careful aim with his Colt Dragoon, and brought him down just a few steps from the woman. She had covered her head, expecting the death blow.

The remainder of the Comancheros ran for their lives, the last one taking a slug in the back from Watt Duggan's revolver.

Emily was now looking up at Jardine, who then squatted down next to her, giving her time to recover and to see that she was now protected.

'It's fine now . . . they've gone . . . they're beat, Miss Nolan,' Jardine said softly, soothingly, as he tapped one of her arms and then stroked her tousled auburn hair. 'We beat them off, Miss.'

'I . . . I owe you my life, mister.'

'Joe. Call me Joe.'

They both knew how close she had come to breathing her last.

Then from behind his refuge in the rocks came Harvey Caldy, holding his lower arm and whining like a starving dog. 'The murderin' heathens – they killed old Snowy. His body's back here . . . and the young man up top!

'Mr Harvey . . . let me see!' Brett grabbed his black bag, which was always to hand, and went to look at the damage done, keen to get to work. There was a considerable amount of blood soaked into his arm, bared when he cut his sleeve. 'No arteries hit, Mr Caldy,' Brett said, holding a pad on the drying blood, 'and the best news is that there's no bullet in there. It cracked your bone and went by . . . but now we fear the corruption of the flesh.'

'Am I going to die? What are my chances of staying this side of the grave, Doc?'

'Well, I think you'll be fine . . . we simply have to watch you closely and be vigilant for fever . . . for sweats and shakes, that sort of thing. I'll bandage it and keep it clean.' Caldy was given brandy and told to sleep.

A while later, when water from canteens had been drunk and bits of food eaten, as they all sat in the shade of the arroyo edge, Jardine and Brett moved the dead men into the luggage boot, covered over.

'So, mister English doctor man, you're going to do what, in this civilized new country? Grow potatoes? Breed horses? Or maybe preach at the stones?' Jardine said, but without a grin, though he wanted to. 'I see that you stuck your knife into this man's neck . . . and look at the condition of your shirt . . . soaked in the man's blood . . . better change, hey?'

'Yes, where is your pantisocracy now, Doctor Brett?' Sir Thomas asked.

There was no reply. But Emily Nolan, distraught and distressed, still felt her arms shaking and her heart beating in her throat. She sat, gathering the strength to keep herself in command of her feelings, and she was strong.

'I suggest we stay here a little while longer' Sir Thomas said, 'and Jardine, would you see to the horses. They suffered, too.' He did so, leaving the

16

others to do their best to return to a normal frame of mind. Time would heal.

There was just enough time to water the horses. But time was also pressing, as Jardine decided they could go on to Bantillo, though the light was failing. They could make it in an hour.

'If we stay here, they might come back . . . and with some more friends!' Jardine said.

Jardine and Watt took over duties on top, and in the stage, Emily, Sir Thomas and Brett sat along one side, with Brett's feet stretched across to stop the corpses from slipping off the seats opposite.

CHAPTER 2

The stage was on the move now. Brett's thoughts ran through all the feelings he had had back home and on the journey across the ocean.

You run and look behind you. Then you find a hole where you might rest easy for a while, but you soon run again, looking over your shoulder. In the end, like a hunted beast, you refuse to take another step and you dig in and fight, wherever you find yourself. . . . You're not immortal and the morrow was not guaranteed . . . now here you are, in this great expanse, going to somewhere utterly unknown.

But he jumped into life again from his doze, and he thought, more confidently, that he would cast away the weight of living, throw the burdens of property and anxiety to the winds, and head out, across that second restless sea, the one of endless earth, the one he should have crossed years back, when his parents died.

He was wakened from his reverie by the sound of Emily Nolan's voice. 'Dr Brett . . . I have never seen death before . . . you must have done. Those men back there . . . seem merely to sleep. But surely their souls are now flying hence . . . going we know not where . . . do you believe in those souls?'

'I'm afraid I doubt in that regard, Miss Nolan. Life has taught me otherwise. These here that we regard sadly, they are but cold containers . . . they were once living beings but now . . . as to any souls . . . I think not.'

'Oh, Mr Brett, shame on you,' Sir Thomas said. 'You must come to my lecture, should we ever reach this God-forsaken town. You must come and hear my reasoning for the life of our souls.'

'I shall come, Sir Thomas . . . you see, I think that the Creator saved us today. He intervened and he saved our lives.' Miss Nolan said.

'I think the man's six-gun and rifle saved our lives, Miss Nolan!' Brett said.

'No, Doctor, my life teaches me differently. Let me tell you about it. It will pass the time while we sit with the dead. You see, my God is perhaps better fitted for my present life than yours!' She said this with a little laugh. 'My parents were German. They were also Jewish, and that meant, if you were only genteel and poor middle classes, you were unwanted. My real name is Noldech. I changed it to sound more Irish! They were kicked out of Munich, my parents . . . Jews who had failed in business you see. He ran a theatre.

They both adored the stage and the acting life. But they were careless with money. They were not among the street-wandering, begging poor, but neither were they inhabitants of palatial residences, as the rich locals were.

'Things would have been fine if Papa had not been tempted to gamble with the small profits from our clothing business . . . the result was that we were soon in a wagon rattling across Europe. And then on board ship heading for Hull . . . then land again . . . and from Liverpool to America. The very name gave me a shiver of excitement. So you see, I come from drifters, poor entertainers, failed middle class . . . yet God has cared for me, I know He has, and He cares for my spirit. Perhaps I have a guardian angel!'

'How captivating you are, my dear!' Sir Thomas said, patting her hand, as a father might.

'Still no proof of any great God taking care of you . . . but you tell a powerful story, Miss Nolan . . . I shall visit the theatre before I leave for the west!' Brett said.

'Bantillo!' Jardine's voice from up top called out. The stage came to a halt and the jumping and swaying motion stopped. The doors were opened, and Sir Thomas shouted to a man standing at a doorway, 'Two bodies here . . . but the living need help, pronto!'

Emily was helped out and her cases gathered. Then the crowd now assembling began to notice her, and newspapermen pressed close, firing questions at her. They knew that she was the new star of the

Starlight Hotel, and when news of her arrival was spread through the streets, there was Kit Lecade, owner of the Starlight, by her side, with his arm around her – and that was a little too intimate, she thought, trying to pull away; Lecade started answering all the questions asked by the crowd. He was in his fifties, thin and dressed like some kind of pretend frontiersman. His long yellow hair was stringy around his neck and shoulders.

Sir Thomas was a celebrity, too. He was met and greeted by the members of the Bantillo élite. A square-set man of around his late fifties approached him, shook his hand, and said, 'I am Padre Burke . . . Alfred Burke. You'll find that folk here call me Doomsday. Welcome to our town, and to the Bantillo Literary and Philosophical Society, my Lord!'

His wife, Mrs Dorothy Burke, was introduced, and then so was Doc Bidwell, the local wiseman, as they all thought him, and finally Sara Jane Dowell, whom Padre Burke introduced as 'Our town bard and rather mystical storyteller . . . she knows every detail of the history of Bantillo, believe me, and she'll write up your lecture for the *Clarion*.'

She gave a cute little curtsey, as if Sir Thomas was royalty, and said, 'Maybe you'll figure in my new epic poem, Lord Rowan. . . .'

'Oh, I'm not a lord, Miss Dowell . . . a mere sir.'

'And I'm not really a miss . . . I'm a widow. Lost two husbands . . . the Lord chose me for one of the lonesome ones, bereft! But I have my poems and letters! A hearty welcome to you, Sir!'

Then there was Harvey Caldy, who wanted to creep away, still feeling so good to be alive. He wanted to get to his family and give them a hug. But Brett spotted him first. 'Mr Caldy . . . it is most important that you have a new dressing on this wound first thing tomorrow. Go to bed and sleep now. Is there someone to care for you?'

'My wife, Doc . . . she'll look after me.'

'Now, if you start to shiver and sweat, send her for me. . . . I should be at this Starlight Hotel. If not, then ask after me. This place is not New York!'

As for Brett and Watt, they took their bags and looked for a room for the night. Jardine, also well known but wisely keeping to the shadows with his one bag of belongings, had his thoughts on the most important subject in his life. He needed to buy a horse in the morning and set about finding a job. Again, he thought, I've been running. All he did, he reflected, was run. It was his one major skill.

Yet he was not alone for long. Charlie Gill, the man who owned the town's paper, knew him well and was expecting him. Charlie was round, squat and happy, with a few double chins and hardly any hair. 'Joe . . . I know what you need . . . no more talk and a few drinks, am I right?'

'You are right, as always. I got a lot to think about.'

'Like what, old friend?'

'Like how a man who's wanting to build a new community . . . all peace and harmony . . . has to stick a knife in someone's throat! Kill or be killed, Charlie. . . .'

'You here to do some killing, Joe? You've done it before.'

'Nope. I'm here to find a stranger . . . the one somewhere in me! Now how about that whiskey?'

'Yes, you deserve it. You got 'em here safe and sound.'

Before they could move away, Dorothy Burke came across to thank Jardine. 'I wanted to express my gratitude in person, Mr Jardine . . . I mean for doing the task so well. Shame about the two men from Galveston. It didn't look so far on the map. We knew it was a risk. But we knew that you were the man to take care of our guest, and you did that real well.'

Jardine gave a quick dip of his head and thought about kissing her hand, but then he remembered she was just a pastor's wife, and shook her hand instead. 'We arranged for the shipping across the Gulf, but after that, well, we asked the good Lord and your guns to see him across the last leg of the journey. The Lord answered our prayers! Now I must go, but come tomorrow at the lecture and I'll have your remuneration ready for you, if that suits you, Mr Jardine.'

'It does, ma'am.'

In the Starlight, Brett and Watt were happy to find that there was a large room available, and in Watt's case, he was even happier to find that Emily Nolan was still visible, now talking to Kit Lecade and to the railroad man, Caldy. But he had to take his eyes off her and carry the bags upstairs.

'She's so beautiful, Leon, that girl.' Watt was still thinking of her. 'That hair . . . and her pretty face . . . I never saw a lady carry off that little lilac dress so well.'

'Wake up and come back to us in the actual world of what is a new Texas, its own self, like it was meant to be. I've been reading about the affairs here, and this remarkable war.' Brett found himself the armchair and sat back, leaving Watt to unpack. 'I've been trying to understand it all. Like most wars, it's a mess, and a strong man is required to resolve it all.'

'But we came out here to forget wars, didn't we? We're heading out soon, right? I mean, when you find the right people for the new beginning?'

'We certainly are, my friend. There might be a war going on, but now, setting foot in this place, so far away from New York, I feel that we've come to the end of everything. What a journey! It's the hardest thing I ever did, covering all those miles down here . . . England is so minute . . . so insignificant, Watt. I mean, if there is to be Liberocracy, then it has to be here! I only wish I could have informed Mr Coleridge about this plan, but he was impossible to locate. Mr Southey, unfortunately, died a few years ago. I did write to him, but there was no reply. I feel that he was rather ill.' Brett was checking his luggage now, and still worrying about his plans as soon as thoughts of them entered his head.

Yet still, although it was growing late, the town was aware of him, and he had forgotten that he had promised an interview for Charlie Gill, owner of the town's paper, who now rapped on the door of their room.

'Leon . . . you said. . . .' Charlie asked, stepping inside.

They were soon sitting face to face in the two arm-chairs in the room, while Watt fixed some beers. Charlie's ample frame filled out his chair, and he shuffled to adjust himself and feel comfortable before taking out his notebook and pencil.

'Now, Leon, my readers want to know, first of all, about the reasons you've come out here, way past the tree-line, into a damned battlefield, when you could be back east tending to boils and bruises?'

'Well now, that's exactly the point, Mr Gill. The last thing a surgeon from London wants is to be no more than a provincial medico . . . not that I would denigrate the profession. The local doctor's calling is a noble one. But I am still young, and I have ambition. I will surely tend to boils and bruises when I'm older, if fate allows.'

'Now, Leon, I have to say this . . . and I don't mean it in a heartless way . . . out here a person has troubles assailing him from all sides . . . many die of pestilence . . . some of bullets and arrows . . . and it's a very long ride to any hint of civilization as we normally think of it. How do you aim to live in these circumstances?'

'I aim to live, Mr Gill, by helping the sick and needy. That is my vocation. I studied for four years in Guy's Hospital, in London, learning to be an apothecary and then a dresser, and finally a sawbones, as I think the plain man calls my work. Surely, of all the places on earth, Texas is in need of a sawbones! But more than that, my friend Watt and I have bigger ambitions.'

'Yes, I have read of them . . . there have been items in the papers back east and snippets have come our way. *The Clarion* is as forward-thinking as you seem to be, young man.'

'I appreciate the compliment. Most people are amused when I speak of my Liberocracy. That is what I wish to establish . . . exactly where is still under discussion. Maybe north of here . . . towards Santa Fe perhaps. But I have come here because I was advised that young men around these parts will spring up and join a new enterprise . . . as they have done when they became volunteers to fight Mexico.'

'Your Liberocracy is . . . ?'

'Well, it's actually the same thinking that inspired your great and young country . . . the land of free men, released from the binding shackles of class that run through British society like a disease. I'm sure anyone moving west or south west from Kansas or Ohio and such places will have a vision like mine, only maybe they think family . . . whereas I think community.'

'You have no problem with the hard facts of the frontier then, as I have described them?' Charlie Gill was enjoying himself. It was an interview like no other he had ever given.

'I have the folly of a young man . . . I'm thirty-five . . . and I have the conscience of a man who sees a world being dragged down by disease and suffering. In fact, as I have learned on my journey, there are plenty of others who want something finer, something more civilized, out here . . . like your Literary and Philosophical Society, who have an English aristocrat in town, preparing, as we speak, to lecture them on something edifying and wholesome . . . something different from cattle or sheep.'

'Yes indeed. I thank you for your time, Mr Brett, and I'll make sure you see the piece I am to write about your . . . your noble enterprise. I think there will be many who need you . . . '

There was a rap on the door and it was flung open. Kit Lecade walked in, hurried and flustered. He stared right at Brett.

'Doc . . . we need you now, downstairs . . . that Jardine character . . . he's damned near killed a man!'

CHAPTER 3

Every man in Bantillo was looking for Joe Jardine. When Brett, Charlie Gill and Kit arrived downstairs, there was a crowd around a man lying on the floor, and he was bleeding severely. Brett told everyone to move out of the way.

'This man is in a bad way . . . what happened?' Brett asked.

'Jardine shot him. They was arguin' over cards as usual. The tall man fired in cold blood. The dead man had no chance, doc.' This was from a solid, heavy man who stood apart, drinking whiskey at the end of the bar counter. It was Sheriff Dan Bowen, and he spat his words out, full of hatred.

'Did you see it then, Dan?' Charlie Gill asked the lawman.

'No, I wasn't here, but I came runnin' when I heard the shootin' and the old-timer there . . . Harry . . . he told me . . . right, Harry?'

The old man in question was in a chair in a corner,

full of beer and sleep. 'Yeah, sure did. Cold, hard murder I tell you . . . that Joe Jardine is a bad man, rotten to the core.'

Dan Bowen made his opinions clear when it came to Joe Jardine. 'That man has it comin', believe me . . . nothin' but trouble since he drifted in here a year back. Word is the man was in the Rangers when he was no more than a cub . . . now he's a full-grown mighty dangerous wolf.'

'But he's known as the Leveller . . . I mean, that's a good thing, surely, Dan?' the newspaperman asked.

'Well no, my friend, far from it. A man like that, he thinks he's above the law. Thinks he's better, in fact. Damned impertinence, if you ask me.'

'He told me he was David up against Goliath. It seems he has a good attitude.'

'Charlie Gill, I always thought you had a brain between them ears!' The lawman was losing his temper a little, and went on, 'A killer is a killer . . . I always thought the man had gone bounty huntin' . . . now that's low as a rattler's belly. Now he's damned near killed a man in my town.'

As he said those words, his deputy shouted out the news. 'Dan . . . he *has* killed a man. The doc says that Rocco's died.'

Brett gave his confirmation as he got up from the floor, wiping blood from his hands.

Old Harry snorted and then wheezed, cleared his throat and told the world in general that it wasn't all bad news. 'Fact is, Rocco Nunez was not exactly one of God's good children. Jardine's taken away one of the Devil's spawn!' He chuckled so that his yellow teeth could be seen across the room.

'It don't matter if the man was Old Nick himself . . . he was murdered in my town, and I want that Jardine in my jail, real soon. Deputy, let's search every building in this place . . . now!'

The crowd dispersed, and the search began. Brett took Charlie on one side. 'Charlie, the folk are saying it was self-defence. A number of them saw it happen. So I was told, at least.'

'Well, I'm sure that's true, but Dan Bowen has been looking for a reason to drag Jardine off to jail for some time now. Let's hope the man has run for it by now.'

'Yes, but I have other things to consider now, Charlie. I have a lecture to give on my Liberocracy . . . tomorrow at five in the Hall. I understand that's where the philosophical people meet. Watt and I need to recruit. It's a long way to the Kimishi river. . . .'

'What? That where you're bound? It's Indian territory . . . all kinds of scum move around there. You met some Comancheros, right? Well, imagine setting down your roots among them! Think again, friend.'

'Yes, but Watt and I, we don't give in so easily. If we can't gather kindred souls around here, we'll find them on the way. We have a few hundred miles to go along the Red River of course.'

'I think you're crazy as a critter chewing the loco root . . . but I have to admire you as well.'

*

When darkness fell and made the streets of Bantillo no more than a place where drunks sang and swore, Emily Nolan was settling into her new home. This was no more than a room at the Starlight. It was compact. She had a bed and a wardrobe, a small table, and enough places for candles so that she could read when she wanted when the bright Texas days had faded into dusk.

Emily had unpacked what few belongings she had and was pleased that Lecade had given her a day to rest before she started work. A general look around had confirmed her expectations – that this was a rough and violent place on the edge of what might be defined as civilization out in this new, young country with its vast open spaces and passionate hope.

She sat down with her novel after kicking off her shoes and undressing. In her nightdress she felt cooler at last, after a tough day. The sweat and dirt of the land had been washed away and now she was back in her story, a tale of a governess in a vast country house, back in the east, where gentlefolk sometimes lived like royalty.

Now here she was in a place where men were killed in hotels, as had happened that day, just hours after her arrival. But her travelling life had inured her to such things. After all, she thought, this was a world just finding out what it was and where it was heading, and most folk were either lost or scared.

Emily had locked her door and did not expect any visitors, but as it grew late, there was a muffled rap on the door and a familiar voice called out her name. She let the voice settle in her head, and then recognized it. 'Mr Jardine . . . that you?'

'Yes, ma'am . . . could I have a word, please?'

She sensed that it would be all right. But his name had been linked to the killing, so there was a shiver running through her body as she opened the door. She knew men – or thought she did, as she had been brought up with brothers, and then working in theatre – so the man's world was not new territory to her.

All she could see was a tall figure wrapped in a slicker, and it had a collar that was bent across his face. His hat came low, and just his eyes were visible.

'Miss Nolan . . . I'm real sorry to come here like this but . . . well, fact is, I'm desperate for a hole to crawl into. There's a hue and cry out there for me . . . and believe me, I have done nothing wrong. I managed to creep up here real quick. Could have been seen easy, but I risked it. . . .'

Emily motioned for him to come in, and then sit on the one chair in the room, but he sat on the edge of the bed.

'They say you killed the man down in the bar.' Emily kept her distance.

'I swear to you, ma'am, it was in self defence. I never took a life just for the evil in it. Now, the lawman in this town . . . he'll have me lynched if he gets hold of me . . . I'm asking for a night on your floor, then I'll be out of town at first light.'

'Mr Jardine, you're asking me to ruin my reputation?' Emily smiled as she said the words. He managed to smile with her. She sat down, gave him a searching look, and considered. 'Why did you come to me?' she asked.

'Because I knew, from when you first spoke in the stage, that you could be trusted . . . you've been tested by life and you've been found to be a winner, that's what I'd say.'

'Would you now? Well, some might say you came to the room of a fallen woman, so one more male visitor would make no difference!' She wanted to smile again, but put on a serious face. The tall man, she knew, had some tenderness in him. He was not able to respond, and her words troubled him. He almost blushed.

'Mr Jardine, I'll either be ruined in the eyes of Bandillo society . . . or I'll be found to have saved the neck of an innocent man. But I do want you out at first light.'

'My horse is out there . . . I can take him and head out soon as there's a streak of orange in that sky. Meanwhile, I see you have eaten?' He looked across at a tray on her dressing-table, on which some slices of bread and cheese were untouched. 'Help yourself . . . and you'll find some whiskey by the bed.'

'I couldn't go nowhere else, Miss Nolan, I swear to you . . . I've too many enemies around here.'

It was a quiet but tense night, and it seemed to last a month, to both of them. Jardine lay his long body across the floor by the window, and Emily lay on the bed, reading. It grew late, and neither was asleep, when Jardine asked, 'Miss Nolan . . . may I ask, are you aimin' to stay around this town? I mean, an acting sort of lady, she should be in a bigger place, surely . . . back east maybe?'

'Mr Jardine, I have a history. All the men in this town know I have. To be an actress is to have affections available for men . . . in particular men out here, who rarely see any woman who might be unattached. . . .'

'Sure. I've seen plenty of those types . . . but that ain't you, ma'am. You're a classy type of gal. Anyone can see that! You're here to be a thespian like, to sing and act along the boards, right? Not to . . . not to throw around, your. . . .'

'My favours?' She came to the rescue. He agreed that it would be a good idea to sleep now. But for most of the night, Joe Jardine lay awake, thinking of how special this young woman was. She was artistic, but she seemed as tough as old steak. She let a man she hardly knew sleep on her floor, and he knew it was wrong to have asked her. But he had been desperate, all right. Jardine had hung around in dark corners, after word got out that the sheriff was after him. They would pin a murder on him soon as breathe. Now here he was, imposing on a woman to save his skin. The thing was, he had known he could trust her. There was an understanding between them. Sure, he had saved her life, and that was a factor, too.

He had never known but the one woman, and she was gone, taken from him. His one time with what the world called a true frontier woman was way back when he was a youngster in the Rangers, and that was Lisa, down in San Antonio. She had become his perfect wife. But fate had her marked down to die young, and the agent of fate had been a short, bullish man, part Apache, a man who put fear into the borderlands. He was said to be related to some chief across by Santa Fe, and he traded in anything that would sell. Drifters and outlaws were drawn to him, like flies to a corpse. Lying in that darkness, hearing the woman breathe and the wind outside flap any loose wood, his mind went to that day when he was told what had happened. He had been away, facing Mexies down by Laredo, and Lisa was left at home, with her brother and their son and the dog. He was told later that the killer had cut down every one of them, and left them to the beasts of the prairie. He had run away with everything in the home worth eating or trading.

Someone working at the ranch a morning's ride down south had said he saw the killer – said he was called the 'Freedom Fighter'. People had seen him and remembered him, as he had a horrific scar across his forehead, betraying the fact that he had been part scalped and somehow survived. The entire bunch of men around him had markings on their arms, or sometimes on their faces.

He would pay, though, one day, the killer. People said he had stone in him, and no heart. Well, one day

Joe avowed he would make the killer bleed, and show the world that he was human like the rest, though he acted like some puma with a leaking wound.

CHAPTER 4

'Ladies and gentlemen, it's such a pleasure to be here in Bantillo, introducing two special guests who will address you fine people of our Literary and Philosophical outfit. In case any strangers here don't know me, well, I'm Padre Tom Burke, and my good lady Dorothy sits down here on the front row. . . .' Dorothy stood up and gave a slight bow and a sweet smile to the assembled citizens.

'Now along this here county we work hard to give Texas a certain culture, an attitude to life that has room for books and ideas . . . we live in a vibrant country . . . we live in a young, new Texas, a place that wins and backs winners. . . .' There was applause now.

'Folks, we have two winners with us tonight: first we have Sir Thomas Rowan, an actual British aristo-crat who has a few acres back across the sea. . . .' More applause followed, and Sir Thomas gave his bow. Tom Burke was sweating now, and he dabbed his forehead with his bandana. 'Then we have a very rare thing – we have a medical man from London, England – Leon Brett. . . .' More cheering and whooping, and finally, when it died down, Sir Thomas took his place by the lectern.

'Ladies and gentleman, Americans, Texans, pioneers, dreamers . . . I come to speak to you of this promised land . . . it is a land where citizens, free of mind and temperament, build a place where man and woman, their labour ceased at sundown, have music, theatre, literature . . . the amenities of civilization. Above all we have our God. He is a good God. He helps those who head out into uncharted land, aiming to make it a patch of the deity's domain. . . .'

He spoke for half an hour, and the Bantillo folk were entranced. After every sentence, Doc Bidwell and Sara Jane Dowell nodded and smiled in agreement. The Burkes looked around the room at the faces, intent on taking in every word from the nobleman from England. Truly, they were thinking, Bantillo would be making the neighbours across the counties, from McLellan to Bowie, jealous of their achievement.

There were questions and discussion, followed by sherry and cakes. Then people took their seats again and Leon Brett stood by the lectern, by the side of the Padre Burke, who said, 'Ladies and gentlemen, this country has always been for dreamers and planners, individuals with big notions of a future . . . Dr Leon Brett is of that stamp. He's here to tell you about that dream, and to hope that some will share it with him. . . .'

Brett was used to public speaking, that became clear to everyone. They listened closely to his account of life in London as a trainee doctor, and then as a surgeon. This was all welcome. But then he switched to his aim to make a new home.

'Folks, I and my friend Watt Duggan aim to actually put these fine ideas of a new and different life into reality. Yes, we know that there have been travellers heading west before today . . . you all headed west, right? You all came steadily from the land back there where there are forests and streams, lots of cornfields and pig-keeping. Well, what I want to do is take the best of civilized life up on to the borderlands, to take my vision beyond the Red River. . . .'

After the last statement, mumblings and muttering were increasingly loud. Finally, the voice of Harvey Caldy called out, loud above the audience, 'Hey, Doc . . . you got an army? By heaven you'll need one, young man!'

Some laughed and some taunted. Brett waited for the hubbub to die down. 'I'll be recruiting in Doaksville, and there I'll get me some armed men. But I'm gathering folk now if I can find the right stamp of person. Anyone here who longs for a settlement where men and women share everything . . . where all wealth is held by all . . . where minds are open to lives beyond the community, then come and see me after this meeting. I welcome men and women with trades, with skills, or even with sheer cussed determination to be a new mind, a fresh attitude, out here where nature bosses everything, and people need to fit in where they can and work with the great Mother Creation.'

'I've heard of dreamers, but this sounds like downright suicide, mister!' came one statement from the back of the room. Other critical words were spoken, but Brett went on regardless.

'Tomorrow I will be purchasing a good, solid wagon, and the day after, I and Watt will be heading up to the Red River. We need people who can work with wood, cook, contribute as a smithy, or as a cattleman. We need men who know the country around Doaksville. But most of all we need those who deeply feel this need to start afresh, to put down roots . . . I thank you for your patience.'

Finally he stopped and sat down, to subdued applause. He waited for anyone who might come up to him with more questions, but none came. He and Watt sat at a table, fussed over by the Lit and Phil folks, but everyone knew that he had his head way up above the dirt of real life. More than once he heard a conversation along the lines of *He'll be dead and shredded in a week out there!* and *Another madman from back home where things is real bad.*

Rowan had preached at them, Brett could see that. Charlie Gill had seen the truth of the Englishman as well – he was a bible thumper, a preacher man dressed up as a cultural business hombre – a type seen more often around east Texas now that immigrants were pouring in, more and more every day from Arkansas, from Tennessee and further.

*

At the other end of town a group of men were gathering at the Golden Guinea saloon, and they were listening to a man who, deep in his drink, was making a vow to the world, drawing close any man who would listen. This was Jiro Serpe Nunez. He was *La Serpiente* to lawmen and rangers, and to many a man in authority. But to the drifters and loose guns he was a character who would bring them plenty of dollars and even more adventure. On this particular evening, he was looking around at every face that stared at him and took in his every word. He was a short, strong man, hard with muscles on his body and harder still with hatred in his mind. His face was swarthy, hairy, and the son of Mexico was, they said, part Apache, and had learned the skills of war with those people.

'You men, you ride with me, we'll have some good time huntin' down this dog . . . this Leveller . . . that's his name I have been told, *amigos*. He's a lawman without the tin star . . . some kind of loco . . . a fool, I say. Well, this fool has killed my brother Rocco, and I loved the man . . . my little brother, stretched out dead . . . and this scum, this tall killer, he's gonna have a slow end to his miserable life, you hear me?'

'He rides alone, Serpe . . . easy prey I'd say,' one of his listeners said. 'Not for nothing do they call you *La Serpiente*, for a snake you are! This man, you will strike like the rattler, eh? You will bite him deep. . . .'

'He rides alone, and he needs nobody. They say

he's a man with no weaknesses.' Another said this with a smile. 'But of course, you can find any man's weakness, Serpe . . . and then strike!'

'Alone? Hey, a strong man, eh? A man who rides alone, he trusts nobody. He is empty inside, like a dried-out skin, like rotten fruit . . . well, this lone man, he's running for his life right now. I'm going after the man, soon as we bury Rocco . . . and yes, I will hit him hard and bite deep . . . who's with me?'

They all made noises that he liked. They patted him on the back. Words were spoken that he wanted to hear. This tall Texan, he would not have long left on this earth.

CHAPTER 5

The next day, before any living thing stirred in the streets, Joe Jardine was at the stables, to pick up his roan where Charlie Gill had kept it for him, letting Jim use his property and his part of the buildings around the hotel. Jardine had nothing in his saddle-bags but some hardtack and his knife and guns. From the straw came the little figure of a boy, who darted towards him and jabbed out the palm of one hand. 'Mister, I watched your things . . . nobody took nothin.'

Jardine had some coins left, and gave the boy some silver. 'You did good, boy. Tell Charlie I owe him!'

With a kick and a soft cluck, Jardine headed his mount out into the country, north east, knowing where the Englishmen were going to be going, and he knew that, for sure, they would have need of him.

He rode steadily at an even pace, out into the

plain; there was a bad mood in him. He never liked taking a life, and even Rocco Nunez should never have died. He had asked for trouble, and he had given Jardine no choice but to defend himself. Now all the plans in his head on the stage journey from the south had drifted away like a flimsy cloud in summer. Here he was again, riding alone, with nothing to do but chew over the events of the last few days. The one heartening thought was that he had been paid up front for the stage protection, so he had dollars to use.

Ahead of him stretched three Texan counties before the Red River. But there was only one track the Englishmen would take if they were going to Doaksville, and he kept alongside that, aiming to sit and wait when he was a safe distance from Bantillo.

The weather was fine, with barely a breeze and a long, open sky. What troubled him was something inside, not anything sent by God to trouble a travelling man. No, it was the woman. It was Emily Nolan that he thought about. But next to her face in his mind was Lisa. How he had loved his young wife, and how deeply he was wounded in his soul when she was taken from him. Years had passed, and he had pushed all thoughts of her from his mind whenever her memory came to him like a shadow across a bright day. But the sadness was tinged with the memory of the joy they had known, and of their son. Everything they had planned had been snatched away.

It had been tough, trying to erase the pain of those memories; he thought of her name, and he heard her laughter, and recalled how she would lay her head on his shoulder as they had walked together. How they had talked and planned, when Texas was finally free and there was hope in the air for a better time to come.

Life had been too full to think of another woman – until now – when Emily had come along. He found himself thinking of her and worrying about her, a young woman alone out there, working with the drunks and cowboys. The trails and the ranches were homes for fugitives, just like him; some ran from the law and some ran from responsibility, but he had been running from himself, from his own desire to avoid any notions of a future.

He knew nothing of it at the time, but back in Bantillo, Emily Nolan was in need of him again.

Emily's first working day at the Starlight had seemed fine at first. She set about tuning the piano in the bar and asked the staff about planning a performance, with a dance included for the men, who longed for a night of drink and dance, and just the sight of a pretty girl. She checked out her clothes in her trunk, and started bringing them out to hang up. But come late afternoon, Kit Lecade asked to see her in his office at the back of the hotel.

He was sitting at a broad old desk, smoking a cigar and swinging back on his chair. 'Come in!' he called as Emily knocked and looked around the door. 'Come in and sit down, you beauty you ... Miss Nolan, you are just the medicine this old wreck of a man needs! Welcome! Sit yourself down right here.' He swung his chair out and invited her to sit on his lap.

'No thanks, Mister Lecade. I don't feel it is appropriate. I'm here to sing ... and to play music. I want to make that clear.'

'Oh really? Where is that written down in your contract? Miss Nolan, I think there has been a misunderstanding here. My letter surely made it clear. There's a lot more to your work here than warbling arias!'

He stubbed out his cigar and stood up, to emphasize his height, so he could walk to her and stand by her. But Emily walked away again, towards the window. 'Mr Lecade, are you saying that my entertainment is to be taken as something more broadly defined?'

'For God's sake, girl! Let's open the window to some reality, right? This started as a cow-town. It still is, partly. But since folks have been pouring in here to settle or to head west, it's grown mightily and the men riding this way ... well, most are on their own. They need female comforts, you understand ... a saloon out here, it's there to see to their needs, if you follow me ... fact is, these young bucks, they got a firmness in their britches and a woman has to be generous to them, you understand?'

'Oh I understand! You mean this is a whore-house and you're employing me as a whore! I should have known that the fancy talk in print was all lies!'

He gave her a long stare, and then sat down again, speaking more quietly. 'Look, the truth is, yes, I wanted a better kind of female. Most women working the hotels and bars out here . . . well, they only have the one talent, and that's lying on their backs and stacking up the dollars. Talk to Martha and Lizzie down in the saloon. They'll put you right. I once did – and it's the truth – want this place to be something more and something better than the usual. I thought I'd cast the net wider and bring in some more culti-vated young women . . . but in the end, a man wants the entertainers here to do a little more than sing sad ballads, and my ladies see the men in my rooms in order to . . . well, accommodate their needs. You *do* see that, Emily?'

Emily Nolan wanted to pick up a chair and hurl it at the man, and one of her hands grasped the nearest piece of furniture, but she controlled herself and said, 'You have made the situation very clear. I will be catching the next stage back east, and con-sider our contract at an end!'

She walked to the door, and Lecade called after her, 'Vacate your room immediately then, you little prig!'

She stamped out and then ran upstairs, her heart ready to burst with wrath and despair. She hated weeping, but there was no stopping the rising sobs that filled her chest, and she was in tears when, walking along the corridor, she met the substantial figure of Watt Duggan, slamming into his chest.

'Why Miss Nolan, what is it? What on earth is the matter? You're weeping!'

'No matter, Mr Duggan, please let me go to my room!'

'But you need some assistance, Miss. May I help you? What has happened?'

He wanted to wrap his arms around her and comfort her, but a gentleman had to allow a lady to rule the situation. She pulled away from him, hiding her face in her hands, and ran off towards her room. He saw her slam the door and go inside.

Watt reported this to Brett when they were together that night, putting together thoughts and plans for the morning, when they would set about leaving town. Brett heard about the poor girl being upset, and then had to listen to Watt go through all the reasons why he should try to help.

'A woman upset has to come out of it in her own time . . . it may all be over nothing of consequence, my friend.'

'No, you're wrong, Leon. It was something of consequence, I know it!'

But Leon had other things on his mind. 'Watt, leave off this for now . . . we have to take stock of where we are. Tomorrow we head out for the north. We have a wagon and four horses, and we have ample food. But look at the response we had at the meeting! Do you feel that we are to fail in this?'

'Leon, look ... this place is too far from Doaksville. By the time we reach there, and the river, things will change. Believe me, the Liberocracy will be achieved! *You* are the one who had to persuade me, so why so faint-hearted now?'

'Ah, it's that meeting! I could see by their faces that the good people of Bantillo were utterly unable to understand what we are doing ... why we are thinking this way ... but you are right, of course, we will not waver ... we leave tomorrow. '

On the floor of the room there were piles of materials and provisions. Watt had helped to gather them, and he now ran through them, writing down a list of what they had. 'This is the farmer in me, Leon. Always know what stock and tools you have!'

There was a knock at the door and a man's voice called his name, and Brett replied for him to come in. Harvey Caldy stood there, looking from one to the other, and saying calmly, 'I wish to accompany you, gentlemen ... nothing is right here ... wrong kinds of minds ... wrong place ... I'm going to Bowie County and looking to make a line to the coast. I take it you need me?'

Brett held out a hand and they shook on their friendship. 'We leave mid-morning tomorrow. Do you have a mount?'

'I acquired one today ... a strong mare. Sir Thomas Rowan advised me. He has been riding since he was a child!'

'It's a time for some whiskey, gentlemen!' Watt said, raising a glass.

'You do know that it's three days' ride to the river? And it's damned wild out there!' Harvey said.

'Of course,' Watt was confident. 'Of course, this is not Surrey, we know that. There are no country gentlemen's seats and deer parks. I bought four revolvers and two rifles today. See this in my belt? This is a Walker Colt. A man can stand against an assault with this and there are six bullets in these chambers . . . very accurate, and lethal. I'm used to firing a scatter shotgun and my father's old musket!'

Harvey screwed up his face as if he was wrestling with a problem. 'My friends, I can see that you are trying to be prepared. You have done your reading, and you have taken advice. But let me tell you that across Texas today there are bandits and outlaws in every mile. You'll see plenty of steers and men swinging lariats. Most of 'em, they'll be on the run or hiding out from the law.'

'But surely there are army forts? We read about them.' Brett said.

Harvey was stunned at the innocence of the remark. 'Mr Brett, yes, there are infantry. They march very nicely, but the Comanche and the desperados across the wild lands, well, they laugh at the men in blue, and that's a fact!'

'Ah, they have no respect for the law? Well, we will take the law with us, along with good, straight morality and respect for other humans!' Watt said.

Harvey could see that the two Englishmen would

50

never see reason on this. Truth would have to slap them in the face before they acknowledged it. He raised another glass and said, 'Well, how some ever, gents, we drink to an adventure!' As Harvey sank his whiskey, he felt a shiver of apprehension at his decision to ride with these dreamers.

CHAPTER 6

Dan Bowen had struggled to find anyone interested in setting out to track down Joe Jardine. He had to face the hard truth that nobody cared much for just another rogue who had blown in with the wind across the county. But of course, the victim had a brother, and as Dan sat with his feet on his desk sipping coffee and thinking of his days in retirement, maybe in San Francisco, La Serpe came in, and he was not in a good mood. He had two men with him whom Dan Bowen recognized as wanted men for a stage robbery, but he said nothing with these odds against him.

'Ah, the noble man of the law . . . doing nothing at all while my brother's killer runs free! Just as I thought. You know, we could do with some proper criminal hunters around here . . . and you're looking at three of them.'

Bowen swung his legs down to the floor and put down his coffee cup. 'Not my fault that there was no enthusiasm for a posse, Nunez. If you three want to be sworn in as deputies and hit out after the man, then I can fix that real easy.'

'That's exactly what I want, hombre,' La Serpente said, holding out his leathery palm. 'Three of us. You give us the tin stars, we are killing the man with the weight of the law behind us.'

'Now just one minute now, Serpente, that is not the law. You bring Jardine back to be tried in a court, with a real judge, and the process of prosecution behind the business. I don't give no tin stars to no bounty hunters, nor men bent on vengeance.'

The two men behind Nunez laughed. 'Mr Bowen, you speak true, of course. I was simply having a laugh about it all . . . of course, we will track the man down, and then . . . if he resists arrest, or if he puts a bullet our way, well, we might have to shoot him down like the stray dog he is. Right?'

All three Mexicans laughed now, and though Dan Bowen looked Nunez straight in the eyes, he knew that there was a hardness there: he knew Nunez was promising to gun down Jardine and bring back a corpse hung over his horse, like a hunter coming home with his kill.

Bowen pulled open a drawer and handed out three tin stars. 'Remember you represent the law of Texas. I have to swear you in. You must raise your hands and take the oath.'

All three went through the empty farce of swearing to carry out all actions in line with the criminal law of Texas, laughing at the words as they spoke them. When they trooped out, slapping each other on their backs and muttering words in Spanish, Bowen knew that he had taken the easy way to carry out his responsibilities. But, he told himself, Jardine was a hired gun after all, and those who live by the gun. . . .

At sun-up, when Brett, Watt Duggan and Harvey walked out after breakfast to set out north, what they saw there made them stop in their tracks and look in complete shock at the sight before them. There was another wagon behind theirs. At the reins was Charlie Gill, and by his side sat Doc Bidwell. Mounted by the side of them was Sir Thomas.

'You have companions, my English friends . . . in the back of this wagon you have Miss Emily Nolan, Padre Burke, Dorothy and Sara Jane.'

'Seriously? The cultural lot are coming along?' Brett asked, his mouth open wide in astonishment.

'Well, we're not part of your great schemes, young man, but we're going as far as Marshal. I'm speaking there . . . and the literary people are coming along for company . . . for a frisk, as the Padre expresses it.'

'By heaven, Brett, we have an expedition!' Watt said, like an excited child.

'Marshal is a day's ride, easy . . . let's git out!' shouted Harvey Caldy.

Watt's mind ran to thinking of Emily in that

wagon, and it warmed his heart to imagine her sweet face. He would take care of her, wherever they were destined to go. What he didn't yet know was that she had a bruise on her face. Before she walked out of the Starlight, Lecade had bawled abuse at her and pushed her to the floor, and her head had cracked against a table as she went over. She told the women of the Lit and Phil that she had fallen on the stairs. Inside her, as she sat in that wagon and tried to join in the small-talk, there was a deep feeling of freedom as she left the streets of Bandillo for good.

Before they could say anything else, Nunez and his friends rode by, waving their hats and screaming insults. 'We go for the tall one! Hope he is praying hard!' Nunez called out. They were soon gone, leaving a cloud of dust behind.

The wagons then followed, heading steadily out to the track going north-east. Charlie Gill, who was going along because he wanted to write up the story for the *Clarion*, made it clear to the Lit and Phil party that this was going to be no Sunday trip to a ranch party.

'Folks, you have to understand this is wild country. There are eyes watching us from everywhere. There could be Indians who have come down from their own lands. There could be *bandidos* out for some blood and plunder. But we got plenty of fire-power now, and most outfits would think twice before they took us on . . . where we have to be real careful is when we strike camp tonight.'

Sara Jane said she had her notebook, and that a good fight would make a wonderful epic poem. The Padre and his wife made fearful noises and referred to the power of prayer. But Padre Burke mentioned that he had a Navy Colt from way back, and he could fire straight if not too nervous. Doc Bidwell, from up front, told the world in general that he had a rifle and a sabre, both retrieved from a battle against Mexico some years back.

'*God help us*,' Charlie Gill said, under his breath. 'There's nobody else who will. . . .'

Joe Jardine had dug in for the night in the first little creek he came across. He found a hole by some cottonwoods, fed his horse, and chewed on some hardtack, his eyes watching the horizon with the keenness of a hunted hare. He knew that someone was after him. He had heard and seen enough disturbance to sense that. He knew that the man he had killed had family. That fact alone meant trouble. The spot he had found had mesquite, and further up the water were tamarisk trees and bare willows, slapping in the breeze.

He had no fire and made no sound. Sitting against a rock, he listened intently, and the night wore on, with just a hint of something on the air – something that made him think of Mexico. If it was the case that Indians were anywhere near, that would be a shock. The word on the trails was that Rip Ford was gathering a very sizeable force of Rangers to head north and look for the nearest Comanche tipis. But that would surely be a lot further north. Everyone you met seemed to know about Rip. If only he would do something about the *bandidos*, the rambling rough-necks out for plunder. They were the real problem in East Texas.

Finally he slept, but he had learned to sleep with his senses still alive, and around dawn, he was jolted into awareness by the sound of voices, and they were not too far away.

Jardine took very little time to be ready for them if they were sniffing him out. He thought that maybe it was Dan Bowen. Sheriff Bowen would sure win some credit if he brought in a killer to face the judge. But a worse scenario for Jardine was that plenty of folks around Texas and up to Arkansas considered him an enemy for settling matters, and for putting right any number of wrongs and grievances. Lawmen did not like ex-cowboys and troopers stepping into their shoes.

But when he moved silently up a slope to get a view above the sound of the horses and voices, he soon saw the situation: it was Jiro Nunez, the Snake, or La Serpiente as his own people thought of him. So, the brother of Rocco, troublemaker and public nuisance, was out for getting even – and worse still, there was the glint of a tin star on his chest, and on the shirts of the two men with him, who looked like the Erita brothers.

Then, no sooner had Jardine felt that he had the men in his sight, than all their heads turned and one of the Erita brothers pointed across to the east. He called out:

'*Comancheros* . . . plenty of 'em!'

The three men were leading their mounts on the lower slope, but now they swung into their saddles and headed south, their heels prodding the horses' flanks as if their lives depended on being several miles away, and real quick, too.

No more than two miles away, down the track, the Brett party had made camp and risked a fire. Charlie Grant and Harvey were taking control, and they expressed no concern, as they had enough firearms to instil some fear into any stray bandits who might fancy their chances of some robbery.

As for Sir Thomas, he was not in a role he was born to take: he could be commander-in-chief, Lord of the Manor, and every other kind of boss a man could imagine. But he settled for striding around the fire where people were keeping warm, and then at the drop-down tailboard at the back of the Brett wagon, which was the makeshift kitchen.

'This wagon,' Dorothy Burke explained as she stirred a pot of broth, 'this has seen more than a dozen cattle trails . . . only up to Kansas, but still, this was the chuck wagon and it's seen some things, I can tell you!'

Watt Duggan was joining in the cooking with Dorothy and Sara Jane – and of course there was Emily, and he had made it his business to look after her. When she had first come into the light when they pulled up, he had seen the bruise on her face and asked what had happened. Dorothy Burke had put in, with rage in her voice, 'Young man, I can tell you who perpetrated this – Kit Lecade, and he should be horse-whipped for what he has done. If you were a real man you would be back there now, cracking a hole in his skull!'

Sir Thomas, with a full knowledge of army procedure after his days in the cadets back home, followed by a few years as a lieutenant in the yeomanry, felt that he should supervise every little move and action; so he walked around, slapping a cane on his thigh, with a revolver in his belt.

'My Lord . . . I mean, Sir Thomas . . . please . . . there is no need to be so military,' Padre Burke begged him, 'This is not Indian Territory. We are a day's ride from Marshal. This is civilization, sir. Marshal has a university. It has male fellowship that pursues the finer things in life. Just prepare your lecture for them, right? I'll see that Charlie and Doc listen out for the thousands of wild savages that you think will descend on us!'

'I'm sure you talk good sense, padre, but let a military man take all precautions, please. This is not the middle of London! Caution is the watchword out here. That I have learned even in so short a time.'

So Padre Burke left him to it, and decided instead to join in consuming the broth and bread that had been prepared. But despite Brett's insistence that everyone should join in the circle to enjoy the feast, Sir Thomas worked out a rota for the all-night sentry duty. Watt Duggan took the first patrol. His mind was fixed on Emily Nolan, and it was not a familiar feeling. There had been no time for such matters in his life after he went from the country down to London, looking for something better than labouring on his uncle's farm. What concerned him was that, as Brett had always said in their talks about the Liberocracy, the colony needed women: it had to have wives.

Watt had enjoyed the company of women in London, but that had been the kind of company you paid for. Everything had been for pleasure, for sheer distraction. Now he looked at this young woman and imagined what life would be like with her to hold and to care for, in a home out in the west, where life would be pure, free of all the greed and hunger for power back in the old world.

Brett was alone with his thoughts as well, and he took over the last watch at the end of the night. Though women had not been on his mind, the struggle for the new colony had, and a sense of failure ran through him. Charlie Grant sensed this unease, and as the first beams of daylight opened up the sky, he walked out, drinking fresh coffee, taking a cup to his new friend. 'Leon Brett . . . dreamer! Here we see the new man looking out across what could be his new empire! That's what I'll write about you, Leon. I'm taking notes! Here. . . .'

They drank their coffee and took in the uplifting moment. Then Brett said, 'This is a wonderful country, Charlie. I can see why you write about it. The only difficulty I can see is that I got it wrong: people might want a new beginning, but they don't want fancy talk and philosophy. Maybe I should merely set up as a medical man and settle for that, do you think?'

'I think that the first men and women who set out from the east into the far mountains, well, they were dreamers and schemers. They sure wanted more than a stretch of land. I think they were poets . . . artistic sorts . . . maybe their poems were in the trees, the grass, the skies. . . .'

'Yes, I can see you as one of the best writers telling the world about Texas and its sense of being a great place . . . I simply feel that I gauged it all wrong. . . .'

He could not complete the sentence. A sound of horses and screaming voices was coming nearer. They both looked up the track and saw Nunez and the Erita brothers riding as if pursued by demons. They came up close, pulled on the reins, and Nunez shouted, '*Comancheros* . . . right behind! Reach for them guns!'

It took only a few minutes for Nunez and Sir Thomas to bellow out orders. Everyone took a gun and went to a position where there was cover. The two wagons were pushed together. The horses were tethered behind where the people stood or crouched. 'Pull whatever cover you can in front!' Charlie shouted, 'Get behind a box or a heap of anything! Make it quick. . . .'

Nobody questioned his words. There was a scramble for positions, and it was now a question of waiting for trouble – but what exactly that was, nobody could tell.

CHAPTER 7

Padre Burke was yelling out his disbelief. 'For Christ's sake . . . this shouldn't happen! We have the forces of law here . . . we have the army!' But these words were said in the midst of chaos. Charlie Gill and Doc Bidwell loaded their guns and took guns to the women, who now lined up behind the Burkes' wagon. Watt took charge of the horses and gathered them behind the two wagons and the members of the party who were squatting down, shouted at by the Nunez posse, who made it clear that there was trouble coming – and fast.

Nunez set up the Erita brothers low on the ground facing the track to the north; he took a position on a rock behind the rest. 'Plenty of 'em, I'm tellin' you, so git low and pray. They're after everythin' you got, and that includes your lives, you follow?'

Sir Thomas levelled his big shotgun from the drop-down tailboard of what had been their chuck wagon.

'Here they come, so fire when I shout the word!'

63

Sir Thomas' voice bellowed out the command like a sergeant major. A shower of bullets raked the first wagon, and everyone cowered low, before rising again and waiting for the order. The riders came in sight, screaming and whooping, some firing arrows which slammed into wood, missing human bodies. Then came the order to fire and the fusillade sent lead into the front rank. Three riders hit the dirt, but the others rode on towards the camp. Doc Bidwell turned to face them, backed up by Watt and Sir Thomas. The Erita brothers got up and ran for cover by Nunez, but one of them was gunned down. Bidwell caught a bullet in an arm and spun around before taking a second shot, which finished him off.

It was when all the attackers had arrived and were circling on their mounts, firing slugs and arrows at the defenders, that Brett saw the figure higher up, behind the assailants. It was the unmistakable sight of Joe Jardine, with his repeating rifle in action, and he had already dropped one man, who fell with a yelp of pain. He then brought down two more mounted men, and ran forward, after putting down the rifle, diving on to a man who seemed to be the leader. He sprang on him and threw him off his horse so he hit the earth hard, and then he sat on him and stuck a knife in the man's breast.

The bullets still cracked into the wagons and the defenders. The Padre was hit and went down, dead as rotten wood. His wife ran to him and clung to his chest. Emily Nolan, now using her handgun more effectively, shot down one of the riders.

But as Jardine sprinted across the camp and threw himself on a half-breed swinging an axe, the assailants decided to move out, and they did so quick as lightning. All fighting and movement stopped except for Jardine and the half-breed, who now wrestled him, with Jardine trying to pull the axe away from the man's grasp. Everyone else stared, except for Dorothy Burke, who was sobbing in her grief: the Padre was dead, and there was nothing she could do. Then Nunez walked across, his hand still grasping his Navy Colt, as he watched the man he had been hunting struggle with one of the robbers. Finally, after a last scream of rage from the man with the axe, Jardine managed to bring one of his revolvers round and shot the man in the temple.

Brett and Charlie Grant walked around the bodies, while everyone else froze in that dark moment of realization that death had invaded their peace; they found Emily standing by the bodies of the Erita brothers, overwhelmed by the fact that there was nothing she could do.

Brett went across to Doc Bidwell, to find that death had taken him, too. There was a heavy silence. They all looked around, trying to take in the sight before them. Nobody spoke, but most went closer to bodies, hoping to find some clue as to the identity of those who had come out of the north to try to snatch their lives away, apparently just to rob them.

Nunez had put away his gun. He went to Brett and Jardine, who had just found Sir Thomas' body down on the dirt beneath the first wagon. He had an arrow in his chest and another through his neck.

'Followers of Juan Bria, the Freedom Fighter . . . they call him the Robin Hood of Mexico . . . I know the picture on this man's arm – see?' He held up an arm of the nearest body from amongst the dead of the attackers. 'See the bell and sabre?' There was a tattoo on the man's arm.

Jardine's heart missed a beat when he heard the words. 'Did you say the Freedom Fighter? That's who these men ride with?'

Nunez turned to give Jardine a long, cold glare. 'That's what I said. He fights under the bell and sabre: the bell is the call to freedom, the sabre is what wins that freedom . . . from the gringo. Most of you deserve to feel his wrath. In fact, Jardine, you are the man I came out here to find. Now, you killed my brother, and so there has to be one more death today!' He let his right hand move close to the butt of his revolver and fixed his look on Jardine. Everyone else moved away.

'Now this man maybe saved our lives today, Nunez . . . and anyway you have a tin star. That means you have to go by the law . . .' Charlie Gill said, his voice threatening. 'You wear that star to keep our peace . . . not to cover your own hatred, mister.'

'There has been quite enough killing for one day!' called out Emily Nolan, who had now walked closer to Nunez, and, though she was still shaking with the effects of the terror that had assailed them, was driven to intervene. She placed herself between Jardine and Nunez. 'You'll have to shoot through me

. . . both of you . . . I'm having no more dying today, you hear?'

There was a moment of tension as Nunez and Jardine kept their hands ready to drop and grasp their guns. But Emily stayed where she was, unmoved. Then Brett joined in. 'Look, we lost our friends today . . . too many of them. Now there's only myself, Watt, Caldy, Charlie, Emily, Sara Jane and Mrs Burke. See over there now – Sara Jane is trying to comfort a woman who had a husband this morning, and is now a widow. Damn it all, now you want more killing, Mr Nunez! Stop this farce now!'

Nunez turned around and walked quickly for his horse, swung into the saddle, and said, 'The day will come, Jardine, when all will be even between you and me!' He jerked his horse round and rode off to the north.

When the bodies of the dead were stretched out in a line, and prayers said over them, Dorothy Burke cracked, and couldn't stop herself from letting out all her feelings, falling to the ground and hitting the dirt with her fists: 'Why does a good God let this happen? I mean, we are good people, and everything we were told said this track was safe. We came for nothing more than a jaunt . . . we were escorting our English guest . . . I mean, why? Why?' She writhed in pain and then curled into a ball. It was Charlie who first went to her and held her, comforting her as well as he could.

'No answer to that question, ma'am,' Jardine said, simply, 'Sometimes fate just moves in and kicks you down in the dust. I suggest we get these into a wagon and somebody takes 'em back to Bandillo. '

'Not me, Mr Jardine . . . I have to press on to Marshal, with Watt here,' Brett said.

'And I have to come with you . . . I am never going anywhere near Bantillo again.' Emily Nolan's face showed that she meant every word.

'Well now,' Charlie Gill said, taking the responsibility of making decisions. 'You ladies should take the dead back . . . Mr Caldy, can you rest easy in the back?

He nodded, and put an arm around Sara, who was trying not to weep, standing over the bodies of her friends. Dorothy Burke started to talk about the dangers of going back, with those savages out there, but she was soon talked down and reassured by Harvey. They could all see that the poor woman was too beaten down to worry too much. Her last words before climbing into the wagon, were: 'If those heathens are waiting for us, well, I'll join my good husband with the angels!'

Caldy said he would get help and be back. 'I'll get Bowen to get a posse together, Jardine . . . just look after everybody. Help will come.' He took charge of the few that were turning back for their own safety, and wasted no time in moving out. The dead were lifted into the Burkes' wagon, and covered over. Caldy took the reins, and Sara sat with him. Mrs Burke sat in the back.

It was early afternoon by the time that Brett and the others set off for Marshal, after an emotional farewell to the others. Joe Jardine led the way; he had taken a bay mare from one of the dead, as his own mount had been shot down. The new mount caused him to feel a shiver of apprehension as he dug in his heels and moved off north. He has always thought, as his father had once told him, that a new horse was a sign of a new life and a fresh beginning. The bond between a man and his animal was strong and heartening, but with a new horse a man had to start work all over again, getting to know his new partner who would carry him and work for him, without answering back, as a man would.

The wagon with the reduced Brett party trundled on behind, and Jardine pushed them from his mind, thinking of how many enemies he had, like Nunez, who might be watching him and waiting to gun him down at any time. But as the day wore on, he had the attackers to think about as well. Where had they gone, and would they be back? Still, a voice inside kept saying, now he knew about the Freedom Fighter and that bell and sabre. Could it be, he asked himself, that the killer he had sought for so long was up the trail? And if he was, it looked as if the Mexican had talked himself into thinking he was with a noble cause, fighting with Juan Bria.

The heat of the day was oppressive, and after a few miles Charlie shouted out for a stop and some shade. When they all walked to the shadow of an enclosed gully and took some water, Brett asked Jardine if the bandits were still around.

'It's likely. They know you have dollars, Mr Brett. They will have heard about your plans, and they know that settling like you plan to do takes an awful lot of money.' Charlie Grant was busy writing in his notebook, not missing any of these speculations.

'Well,' Jardine continued, looking at the horizon, 'We got another night out here, and a long day after that to Marshal. I'll do my best to keep you alive and your dollars with you in your saddle-bags. But after Marshal, well, I got plans of my own, which involve finding the man who leads these scum.'

It was Watt who responded to this. 'Mr Jardine, I think that Brett and I would like to change your mind. I mean, wouldn't you agree, Leon, that Joe Jardine is exactly the kind of man we need to get us out into the borderlands?'

Before Brett could answer, Emily squeezed Jardine's hand and smiled at him, 'Oh yes, Joe Jardine, take the job. I want you to stay with us, please!'

Watt saw this and felt a surge of jealousy in him. The girl liked Jardine, and maybe more than *liked* him.

'You mean, you'll hire me, Mr Brett? As a scout?'

'We can call it a scout. Will you take the job?'

Jardine looked at Emily, and he couldn't say no to her. 'Sure . . . the Freedom Fighter can wait, I guess. But only as far as the Red River. Anywhere north of that, you need an army with you.'

'Then we have a reason to raise our cans of

water. . . .' Charlie Grant said, lifting his can, 'To the Liberocracy! Five of us now, but fifty when we reach the Red River, right?'

'Right,' said Brett and Watt, together. They were skilled at convincing themselves, but it was a tougher task to convince others. And inside his own mind, though he would never admit it, Leon Brett was finder it tougher to ratchet up the faith in his mission with every day that passed. But he would have to find the words, and find the right sort of people to bring into his frame of mind. He could see the doubts in the eyes of those he tried to convince of the vision, and he could sense, more and more, that what he wanted to say, and how he said it, was maybe too much like a preacher, crazy for converts – and that never did achieve anything. He had seen all that 'God talk' evaporate into nothing when Sir Thomas had ranted.

Jardine was the only one who noticed the glint of sunlight up above them, along the trail. Somebody was watching them, and it wasn't a picnic party out for a good time. He had to pin his hopes on Caldy. Would the man do what he said he would? How long would it take to ride back to Bantillo and then have Bowen shift himself from his comfortable office and assemble some useful gunmen? No, he would have to trust nobody but himself, as usual. In the end, a man had to trust in the faith he had in himself, and in the quality of his weapons.

Somebody was watching them right now, and whoever it was would have a massive advantage. It was time to dig in, to watch for anything that moved, and react quicker than whoever it was out there who might be expecting some easy prey.

CHAPTER 8

The party rode on north, slow and easy. They were all worried, naturally, and eyes kept scanning the skyline for movement. But it was strangely peaceful and quiet, and Jardine was troubled by that. He kept his rifle handy, ready to pull out from the leather, and he had his two handguns. Ever since his Ranger days, he had kept up the habit of always carrying a rifle and two Colts, along with hardtack and water. These gave him the best assurance of survival out in the wild lands he had known so well.

That thought, about his days down in the Mexican lands, living every day in a lawless chaos, made him think hard about the situation now, because it was against common sense and reason that the Freedom Fighters would be this far north of the usual homeland they treasured so much. Maybe they were a maverick band, or maybe even an outfit that had broken away, he thought. Were they loyal to Bria, or to anyone? That tattoo didn't make you a soldier in that particular army. It could just as easily make you a renegade. Chances are, he thought, they could have some kind of alliance with the Comanche – and that was not so rare.

Jardine rode on ahead, scouting, winding around the wagon and taking in the lie of the land. But back on the wagon, folks were ready to rest up when dusk drew on, and Watt Duggan took his horse from the back and rode up to join Jardine.

'Mr Jardine, the general feeling is that we camp just up there, see the little patch shaded by the over-hang?' Watt came up alongside and looked at the tall man, waiting for a reply. At last it came, after a while when Jardine was chewing over the thought in his mind.

'Well, young fella, if you aim to increase your chances of being taken back in a cart for burial in Bantillo, then do that.'

'Mr Jardine, do you take some delight in being surly? Or maybe this is a frontier habit? I mean, manners are strangers to you, I think. You seem to inhabit a dark country all of your own making, and you rarely peep out to see reality.'

'You one of these eastern philosophers, like that set of crazed souls in Bantillo? I thought you were a man of the land.'

Watt took the opportunity to drive in some more doubt, or so he thought, into the hard shell that covered the man. 'So I'm right . . . you have no inter-est in civilized behaviour?'

Jardine laughed out loud. 'Civilized behaviour? Mister, you cultivate that, and you're booking an

74

early grave, out in the desert some place.'

Watt hated being ridiculed, and he could see from Jardine's face that he didn't rate him at all. His next words backed this up. 'Mr Duggan, you want to settle out here, you slough off the good manners, the afternoon tea and chatter, right? You learn how to use your fists and you learn how to shoot straight. Handling a knife is handy, too. Most of all, don't trust nobody.'

'You are a philosopher then?'

'I like to think I'm wise.'

'Well, it would be wise – if I can take my turn in giving advice – if you took no interest in Miss Nolan.'

'Who says I am?'

'Ah, she likes you, and that's clear to anybody. But the truth is, I find my affections tending that way, as I'm a captive of her eyes and her beautiful spirit.'

Jardine laughed again. 'Well, you city folk, you sure churn out some pretty words. Wish you gave the same attention to the scenery. . . .'

'Scenery?'

'Yeah . . . like that mounted man ahead, just sliding a little down a slope. He's been watching us for the last mile. I think we will camp here, but on the left side, a hundred yards in, close to the rock side. Go tell them that, Mr Duggan.'

They were soon camped and eating what they could dish up from their supplies. They had coffee, and that was a welcome reward after the day's labour. When the horses were secured, and the wagon taken in so it touched the rock wall, Jardine gave his warning. 'Folks, we are being watched . . . could be the same crowd again that hit us yesterday . . . or it could be Nunez. It's dark enough for me to get around the back and see what I can see. Charlie, you're in charge. You hear any gunfire, don't react. Don't run to it, you got it?'

'Sure. I'll stand at the back of the wagon. We'll have a night shift.'

Watt thought that he had taken care of any rivalry in speaking out. At least, there had been no reaction to his warning. He took the chance to spend some time with Emily as they sat by the warmth of the fire, and the men took the conversation on to the topic of Liberocracy again. Leon Brett was trying to persuade Harvey to join him.

'Emily . . . Miss Nolan, could I ask, are you planning to stay in Marshal?'

'Why yes, I heard from Mrs Burke that it is very advanced . . . there is a great deal of education going on there, and musical performances.'

'Are you a Thespian, Emily? Do you tread the boards? Have you played Shakespeare?'

'You do fire your questions, Watt Duggan. Give a girl a chance. Yes, I would adore the chance of playing the Bard. I'm told that there is an acting company there. I can play piano for them, too, if they need me.'

He was sitting close and admiring her hair as she spoke, as the firelight flickered on her forehead. He could tell from her voice that she was a performer. Never, not even back in London, had he ever met a woman like her, and his soul was stirred. He wanted to hold her and kiss her. But of course, he had to hold back and say the right things. But most of all he listened, until there was a pause, and he said, without really thinking about his words, 'Emily . . . you ever thought about settling down?'

'Oh, you mean being a wife? Goodness no! I am too ambitious, Mr Duggan.'

He was blind to how she was really feeling, and that was something he would never want to know. She thought of him as too rough, too unschooled. In her book, he was no more than a lively colt, and if she ever needed a husband, she would need a certain maturity in her man.

When some food was prepared, most of the party started to unwind a little. But Jardine, after taking some coffee and soup, went back to sit above the wagon and keep watch. Charlie, his notebook out again, asked Brett if he was giving up on his new community.

'Mr Gill, I'm disappointed in you, sir! Yes, we had a setback. Yes, things look a little bleak just now, but believe me, I am more than confident that we'll bring in fresh minds in Marshal. I read about the place . . . people pouring in there every day . . . there's a fort fairly close, and immigrants drifting across from Arkansas and further, all the time. '

'Sure, I heard the same, but I'm still not too clear on what you're offerin', like.'

Watt intervened now. 'Mr Gill, when I first met Leon here, I was lost, and wandering London. Now that's a pitiless town. Over in England, people on the land are being thrown off, forced out to scrape a living in factories and in mills. It's a country where you work or die. That teaches a man hardihood and a hunger for something better . . . I suppose all these people streaming west are like me in that respect.'

'Sure, but they ain't all dreamers. Some folk have a sense of reality. I mean, where you're headed . . . it's teemin' with savages. You read about the Indians, Mr Duggan? No? Well, let me tell you that they can outfight the best we have. The truth about this corner of Texas is that the army is puttin' in troops who march around all nice and perdy, in their neat wooden forts, but out there . . . out up north and west mostly, from the Red River, there's men who ride horses into war, better riders than any you got back home. . . .'

Jardine came to the fire to help himself to some coffee from the pot left hanging over the heat. He felt that now was the time to say something that he wanted to get off his chest. 'Brett, I agreed to help you move on and maybe survive, but I have to say that I've always trusted what I can see, what I can feel, the earth and the wind, the animals I worked with, and my own sweat. Never was one for imagining some kind of paradise here in this fallen world. . . .'

'Well, Mr Jardine,' Brett responded, 'I can understand that attitude, but you might as well be a gopher, digging in the dirt, than a man, seeing the world like that . . . look to heaven, man, and look over the horizon.'

Jardine now drank his coffee, but his eyes were still looking around, ready to react to anything that disturbed the peace. 'Oh, I've done that, mister. I've dug in and chewed wood like any old prairie dog. Times have been so hard that I done the work of a mule . . . life out on the frontier don't leave no time for too much philosophy, though I learned that too . . . from an old-timer when I was out working the coast by Galveston. I know that a man has to think, and yes, I look to something further than the horizon . . . but I'd say you didn't plan before you left Bantillo . . . never did a thorough survey of what lay ahead. . . .'

'Well, now we have you to guide us, and I feel a lot better about things,' Emily added to the talk. Jardine said no more, and walked away.

'The man perhaps has a point,' Brett said, but Emily tried to comfort him. 'It's not your fault that people died . . . you weren't to know about these devils out here, looking for blood . . . God only knows why they came at us . . . they must think we have gold in the wagon!'

'Well, there might not be gold, but there are a few thousand dollars in my bags,' Brett said. 'They could merely want the wagon, and everything we possess that's stacked in there.'

'Ah, we'll worry when trouble comes,' Watt said, refilling his coffee cup.

Brett felt that his brain was being challenged, and so he gave a lecture on how wonderful the future was going to be up the Kimishi River. It was time, Charlie thought, to go and talk to Jardine.

Jardine had gone back on watch, and had been surveying the lie of the land before darkness fell. He always did. When Charlie arrived and sat by him, he gave a report to the one other person in the party who would understand. 'Charlie . . . behind us here there's a mighty useful *arroyo* . . . did you notice the stretch of mesquite? It goes back around half a mile, right to the canyon mouth. The tree stand above the brushwood gives good shade and cover . . . if we need to, we can use that space.'

'Do you think we'll need to do that?'

'Who knows? We might get through the night, pack up and move on, and reach Marshal by nightfall. Then we got some peace of mind. But you know these Comanchero lot – they hate a defeat, and they let their vengeance burn into them.'

'Yeah . . . and do you think Nunez will have left?'

'I'm uneasy about that Juan Bria connection, Charlie. Why in hell's name did that attack ever happen? I guess that the Rangers have moved north. Where else would they go?'

'Fact is, Joe, nobody cares enough to bust a gut and come out to see for themselves. Too fond of the stink of home and the beauty of leaving men like you to face the trouble. Seems to me you *like* trouble. . . .'

Jardine allowed a smile. He liked Charlie, and spoke freely to him. 'You gonna write some fancy words in your book, Charlie? Don't make me into no damned hero, you hear? There's characters driftin' around east Texas who want me dead . . . I got more enemies than there are flies in a butchery.'

'I'll write that down . . . when I can get to a candle,' Charlie joked.

'Well, I have no cloudy notions of settling down with the crazy Englishmen, that's for sure. I guess I didn't have no definite ideas of the future . . . until yesterday.'

'You mean Nunez?'

'Yep, Charlie . . . that tattoo . . . I've had bad dreams about that bell and sabre – for years. Now I get the sense I'm closing in on a little satisfaction. You see, Charlie, most of my life I been putting right what the law don't fret about. But that's been for other folk. Now I got somethin' to put right for me. I think Nunez knows where the Bria band are to be found.'

Charlie's attention was diverted from his friend's face before he could give a reply. 'Joe . . . movement . . . over to the right, behind you. I saw a white shirt!'

There was a thump in the trunk of a willow behind Charlie, and both men sprang to their feet and sprinted to the wagon. It was the sound of a bullet.

CHAPTER 9

Jardine wasted no time in racing back to the others, shouting at Charlie to get to the wagon. 'Get the horses hitched up, real quick, and then drive it straight up through the brushwood and under the mesquite . . . see the gap in there? Take the wagon through and right up to the rock face.'

As Charlie went to follow these orders, Jardine hissed more commands at the others, who were still talking around the fire. He kicked dust over the flame and put it out, then snapped out, 'They're back . . . must be the Bria lot, anyways . . . now on your feet, pick up weapons and bags . . . and follow the wagon . . . *now, now*!'

They were soon squatting in a line in the brushwood, backing steadily into the depths of the mesquite. There was just enough moonlight to see the tops of the boughs, and some of the plants were lower than others, forcing them to duck. Their movements were seen, and some bullets came at them, though they were wide of the mark.

Ten minutes later, Jardine made out some movements down at the arroyo's mouth. He could see mounted men, maybe around twenty of them. 'Now git low . . . squat down under the mesquite, have your guns ready and watch the other side of the brushwood. They can only come at us from that one place, see? We got the advantage. We don't have to move one little toe. But they got to come at us. They know the light is ready to spread out and show movement . . . and maybe they'll rush us then.'

Watt was close up to Emily, lying under the wagon, and Charlie was under a mesquite canopy, twenty feet away. Brett was with Jardine, ten feet above, behind a mesquite top, on a ledge of rock. Jardine looked around and he saw that the others had old handguns, and one rifle, in Watt's hand, and he thanked his guardian angel, which he had always believed in, that he had his Walker Colt. If they rushed the grove of mesquite, the Bria outfit would be easy targets. They might run off like last time if too many fell.

There was silence for a while, and the light gradually began to fill the skyline with an orange glow. The quiet was disturbed by the first animal calls of the day, and a few creatures disturbed the undergrowth, making everybody's nerves twitch.

Then a voice called out to them. '*Buenas Dias,* Texans! General Muntara speaks with you! The war is not finished, *amigos* . . . we fight for Mexico . . . all we want is the wagon and the money. Soldiers of Juan Bria never break their word . . . ride away and leave everything, and no more killing, *sí*?'

'The war is over. You need to accept that, mister. You think we left our brains back in Bantillo?' Jardine called back. 'We can't trust a man who wanted us dead yesterday. Go, and go right now!'

There was a cold, tormenting laugh from the Mexican. 'Oh yes, of course, we will leave you alone because you ask so politely! Now ride out . . . or die!'

'You got to prise us out . . . we got shade and you got warm air. It's likely to be real hot, and we got some hot lead. Ready to burn, general?'

'I know you, Jardine. I will enjoy burying you in this stinking nowhere!'

The general's voice rang out a command and a volley of bullets slammed into the mesquite. But the hot lead hit the dirt, falling short of Brett's party in their shade.

There was quiet again. Brett called out, low and with fear in his voice, 'Mr Jardine . . . what will they do?'

'Maybe ride at us . . . he's got men to spare now.' Jardine had figured out that there were more Comancheros in the general's troop than before. There had to be some kind of camp or base fairly near.

From the edge of the arroyo, a line of the Bria men rode their horses into the brushwood, and they were slowed down; they were aiming to fire from the side of their mounts, swinging down from their saddles. 'Some of these men are Comanches I think, or Kiowa!' Jardine shouted. 'Don't fire yet. Wait for my call. They'll drop down out of your line of fire.'

The horses slowed, and some reared up on to their hind legs, and their riders fired from all angles. There was shouting behind them as the general snapped out his commands. Muntara was running left and right behind them, with some of his side-kicks, yelling and screaming above the noise of the horses and the gunfire.

Jardine shouted for everyone to fire now, and then he wasted no time in jumping down and moving while crouching low, then dived into cover and fired from the dust. He picked off two riders. Behind him, Charlie and Watt were being too bold, standing to see their targets better. '*Get down!*' he screamed. But Watt, now too bold, took some steps forward and he was hit in the shoulder. He went down, clutching at the pain.

Muntara's voice was heard above the racket, and his men turned and rode back, out of range. As they ran, the defenders went to Watt, Brett reaching him first. 'Watt . . . let's see . . .' He tore the shirt where the bullet had entered and assessed the damage. 'Watt, you idiot . . . you gave them a good broad target to aim at and they didn't ignore the chance!'

'Sorry, Brett . . . damn fool I am! It does hurt.'

'I think it missed anything crucial. Emily . . . could you stay with him please . . . keep this clean pad on him . . . the bullet is still in there. Let's lift him to cover . . . Charlie, help me!'

Jardine kept watch as the others carried Watt to some good cover. It was hot now, and the sun was punishing anything that moved out of the shade; it stayed quiet for a while as Jardine fixed his look on the far side of the brushwood. All he could hear behind was the groaning of the big Englishman. Jardine's mind was figuring out the options available to the general. These were a strange band, he thought. They were fighting for Bria, that was for sure, but they were a long way from the border, or even from the Gulf, where they might have had a vessel in support of their raids.

Then there was the question of the Rangers. Word was that they were riding around the county, taking care of the settlers as well as the folk who were already fixing to put roots down into Texas. So where in tarnation were these men? When he signed up to guide Leon, he had thought it would be an easy job, with no sign of any trouble. Again, as so many times before, he was wrong. Now out there, staring at him with an intent to string him up, were a bunch of wild men who were hungry for the dollars back there in the saddle-bags.

He decided to sprint back, running zig-zag through the brush and then under the shade of the mesquite. There was Watt, lying flat, with Brett over him, and Emily pouring whiskey into the big man's mouth.

'I have to take the bullet out, Watt . . . this will be painful. Have another drink.'

'Yes, Mr Duggan . . . take a good pull of this. . . .' Emily said, leaning over him. As for Charlie, he now had his rifle cocked and ready to fire, and he was spinning around, watching every inch of the surrounding bluff.

Brett slid his pincers into the running wound, and Watt gave a piercing scream, coming out of the depths of his hurting soul. Emily put a length of wood in his mouth for him to chew on in between his groans of agony.

Jardine and Charlie stood back, waiting for the slightest sign of movement down at the other side of the glade of mesquite. 'What's he gonna do, Joe?' Charlie asked, nervous.

'I wish I knew. He can't charge us . . . maybe they'll sneak in, bellies rubbin' dirt, like sidewinders. . . .'

Then it was done: Brett held up the pincers, which gripped the slug. 'Give him some more whiskey, Emily,' he said. She did just that, and held up his head with one hand; Watt managed to hold the bottle and take some drink. He was sweating, and falling in and out of unconsciousness now. 'You know, good friends . . . you know, he's a wonderful medic, this friend of mine . . . he saved my life before, in London. Yes, saved my life. I had been beaten and robbed, left for dead in a stinking dark street, by some stinky bastards from the slums . . . but along comes the young . . . young medical student . . . the apoth.. apoth'cary . . . .and he saves this carcass o' mine.'

'Enough, Mr Duggan . . . I want you to sleep now,' Emily said, with comfort in her voice.

It was Charlie who saw the firelight. He yelled out, 'The devils are gonna burn us out . . . look!'

87

They all looked to where he pointed, and they saw some men throwing burning sticks into the dry brush.

'Right,' Jardine said, 'There's not a second to lose . . . everybody into the wagon. Get Duggan in first. Pick up your guns and bags, right now . . . get in that wagon. Charlie – get the reins. We're gonna drive through that brush before it reaches the mesquite . . . if we don't get through that fire, we'll die here!'

There was a scramble. Jardine picked up Watt, with the help of Brett, who held his friend's legs, and they put him in the wagon. Charlie hitched up the horses, then jumped up to turn the thing round, facing the burning brush. Emily followed, and then Jardine threw the last items inside, and went to mount his horse. This was a mighty big risk, he told himself. 'Get movin' right now, Charlie . . . Move it out!' He screamed as loud as he could.

The attackers were taken by surprise. They had expected no resistance, and the smoke now coming from the burning brush was dense. But Charlie, at the reins, looked ahead at the dark figures moving around at the far side of the smoke, and cracked the whip over the two sturdy team horses he knew so well by now.

Behind the wagon, Jardine showed he could ride Comanche as well as any of the general's men: he dipped to one side and fired his Colt at any human shape moving within range. The danger point came when his back would be facing the Comancheros, as the wagon raced away; Jardine swung around, riding by his horse's neck, and praying that the bandits wouldn't shoot the animal to bring him down. They did try, but the visibility was poor, and there was soon a considerable distance between the general's killers and the wagon.

Jardine was soon riding up close to the wagon, which started to slow now. He could hear groans and strange words coming from the wounded man, and he could hear Emily's voice offering comfort and reassurance.

When he rode close to the front he told Charlie he could slow down now. 'Nobody following . . . they've given up on us this time, my friend! You did a fine job . . . forget the newspaper line of work and start a stage company!'

'I prefer to fight with the pen, but I sure am glad I got this rifle from a no-good drifter who owed me something from a card-game!'

'You did well, Charlie. You're as useful with a gun as you are with a pen!'

'Joe . . . be straight with me. Do you think that Caldy will make it back here? Will Bowen come?'

'Charlie, all I know is that Harvey Caldy seems like a reliable type. I'm not concerned about him. It's the lawman who worries me. Too selfish. He loves only himself, that man. What's he got to gain by rousing up a score of gunmen and comin' out here? Maybe I'm turnin' mean spirited now. Maybe I lost my sense of trustin' and havin' faith in folks.'

'Well, if that's so, you're joinin' my club, Joe. Scrapin' up news means that you tend to think the worst of humanity. I guess I lost any dregs of faith I once had, too, and it's all down to chasin' up stories of men turned nasty. But then you look to someone like Emily Nolan, and you see a good woman. I can believe in her.'

Jardine wanted to agree. He had a lot inside him about Emily that he could have said, but this was not the time and the place. He settled for a nod and a simple agreement. 'I'd trust her, Charlie . . . I would trust her. She's a good woman!'

They moved steadily onwards, everyone silent except for the injured man, and Brett was praying that his friend would soon sleep. Watt himself was only a little aware that Emily was the one caring for him, and many times he called her 'mother' when he spoke from the madness of his delirium.

'How's the patient?' Jardine called from his horse.

'Wild and raving, sir . . . his mind has gone . . . for now!' Brett said.

Jardine thought that his mind had gone too, when he wondered why he had said yes to this dreamer – but at least the man could do his doctoring.

CHAPTER 10

They reached Marshal at sundown and Watt was taken to a hotel, where his wound was cleaned and his bandage replaced; then he was left to sleep. Brett told everybody that he would pay for their rooms – but what more he said as the travellers all gathered in the bar of the hotel came as a shock.

'Fact is, if I pay for the rooms and the stabling, well . . . then I have no more money! I'll have to try to get a loan. I was hoping that when the dollars ran out, I could be in the new country and be growing my own food.'

Jardine looked on him with pity, and Emily with complete shock – but Charlie took out his pocket book and checked how many notes he had.

'Charlie . . . if you publish this, I'll be a laughing-stock!' Brett said.

'Take it easy . . . I wasn't noting your dire circum-stances! No, I was seeing how much cash I could offer you. Not enough, is the answer. But no, I wouldn't make you look a fool . . . though I *am* writing up your story, we agreed on that. Now, though I'm short of dollars, there is help here. The Burkes and their Society are not without friends, Doc, and they're my friends too. I'm sure I can have a word with them and find you some help.'

'That's magnificent! You are a true friend, Charlie Gill!' Brett shook his hand. 'You see, both Watt and I were not exactly rich, back in London. Far from it. He was, as they say, in the gutter. I had been saving for a few years while working at the hospital, and I saved quite a lot. But now it's run out . . . if we could have a few nights here, then I could recruit and soon be at the Red River.' He turned to Joe Jardine: 'Mr Jardine, can I still count on you to lead us?'

'Well, until the general and his no-good robbers set about us, I would have said no. But now I need to track them down . . . find out who took away my family. I'm nearer now than ever before. Truth is, I'd given up hope of findin' the devils, and then along comes this crazy rebel.'

'Now, does that mean you're with me still? Though at the moment, I couldn't pay you, Jardine.'

'It means that I'll come along up beyond Red River, but we'll be easy prey for any number of *bandidos* and troublemakers. And it seems to me that your wagon will most likely attract the kind of rattlesnakes that look for the innocent types that walk into their grasp. I'll say yes, but I'm a damned fool.'

*

Later, when they were settled into rooms, Watt lay in bed in the room he shared with Brett, with Emily by his side, giving him a warm drink. He had developed a fever and could not lie still. He raged and tried to flail his arms around, but she managed to give him some sips of hot tea in between the fits of shouting.

Time went on, and he slept for a while, but it was fitful. He would wake and speak nonsense, then reach out his arms and try to hold her, but she pulled away. But Emily felt good, being needed. After the failure at Bantillo, she had joined Brett in desperation, then was slowly beginning to see that Brett and Duggan wanted her as their first female settler. It was not a good feeling: there was something worrying about the two men and their passion for a new life, and just now there were no other women drawn to their enterprise. Maybe, she thought, they were just two more men with more fancy thoughts and notions than hard common sense. But still, she was wanted, certainly by Watt, and after hours of tending to him and watching him cope with the shivers and torments of fever, he finally sat up, and seemed to realise properly where he was for once. And then he said, 'Emily Nolan . . . you know how I feel about you. . . .'

As she listened, looking him straight in the eyes, Joe Jardine was walking up the stairs to the room, aiming to check on the patient, and, more importantly, to see Emily. He had been watching her from a distance since that night in Bantillo, and now

93

there was something inside him, urging him to be with her – no more than that. Something inside him was bothering him like never before, and it related to how he felt about the girl. With every step he took on the stairs he thought about what he might say to her. *Joe Jardine*, he said to himself, *you know that being lonesome out there . . . it won't do . . . admit you need someone.* Then, as he reached the landing, with Watt's door half open, he heard the man's words to Emily:

'You are the kind of woman a man needs out here, my dear. . . .' Watt was saying, 'I'd like you to partner me in the New Paradise, as I like to think of it. . . .'

'Partner you? Watt Duggan, are you proposing marriage to me?' Emily said.

Watt's voice changed a little. He stuttered the next words, but finally said, 'Well, I know that I can't contemplate living out here without you by my side. . . .'

It was more than enough for Jardine. He turned and went back down the stairs again, his heart sinking. When he reached the hall downstairs, he looked out at the door and the broad street outside. There was nothing to say or do. The woman was taken, spoken for. She had a man. He had left it too late, as he had always done. There was a yearning inside him now, for the only thing that would help: whiskey.

There was no sign of Caldy, or Bowen either. It was too much to hope that Caldy had got Bowen in Bantillo and then picked up more men – maybe even a posse if he could be persuasive. . . . That *would* be an army. Then they could all ride on to the river with plenty of protection.

But that was a pipedream. He was still on his own, taking responsibility for everybody. But at least, now they were in a town, with a sense of safety, he could take a drink or two without fretting that the defences would be down and some murderous Comancheros would come sneaking up to them with knives drawn.

Jardine always managed to find reassurance in himself, though, and this time the whiskies helped. He had always stood alone, at least since he had lost Lisa. In his drink, feeling sleepy, his mind wandered into a state of being half awake – a time when memory was opened up like a rotten carcass. He saw Lisa's face in this half dream, her lovely face coming close to him, on a summer's day, with a breeze whipping strands of her long hair across her face. He saw the freckles across her nose, her beautiful pale grey eyes . . . and then there were other pictures, scenes he dreaded. He felt himself walking into the room where her body lay, alongside her young brother. Two lifeless young people, lying there before him, and him helpless. He saw his own face, his eyes welling up, and the sobs wracking his body. Then his fingers covered his eyes and Lisa's dead face faded away again.

Charlie Gill was right about Marshal being a place where the Burkes had some influence: sure enough, one visit to the grandest church in town meant that the Lit and Phil crowd's partners were interested. Charlie took Brett to meet the local leaders, while Emily stayed to look after Watt, who was still in some pain. As for Jardine, he saw that the horses and wagon were well taken care of, and then went to find a card game, and that drink.

Jardine was about to enter the Red Diamond when all the people walking around turned to the east, responding to the noise on the road: it was a party of folks coming to the town. An old-timer sitting around the bar's walkway told Jardine what was going on: 'It's more folks looking for a new life. They been pouring into east Texas for months . . . seems like this is the Promised Land. I seen Germans and Norwegians . . . and slaves running away for freedom . . . I seen single wagons and lines of maybe ten . . . they all think that Harrison county is where they'll find their dreams fulfilled, mister.'

Jardine watched them pass: maybe forty of them, with three wagons, a dozen mules, and a visible portion of hope and fear in their eyes. They were like Brett, he thought, there was that same look in their eyes, like they were in some kind of trance. He admired the single-minded attitude, but they were sure open to being mightily wronged and exploited. Now here he was, sticking with a loser, if ever he saw one, and this was a loser who couldn't even pay him.

It would have been all right if he could have been with Emily. He saw now, after searching inside himself and really understanding why he had strung along with the Englishmen, that it had all been for the girl. Now he had lost her. Once, one of his old partners, Larry Two Wolves, a man who stopped a Mexican bullet at Laredo, had said, 'Joe, my old *amigo*, in the end, your one reliable friend is a bottle of the golden juice . . . it's for the journey to the best destination: oblivion!'

Oblivion, he thought. *Oblivion*. He let the word run around his head. He liked that word. He liked it so much that he thought he would take some other *hombre* with him to that desirable destination. He would drink to his old partner, Larry Two Wolves. The truth hit him hard: Larry was half Comanche, and had some beliefs that he tried to explain. That had been a struggle for Jardine. He wanted life to be something easily explained. Now he was starting to believe that it was not, and never would be, that simple. A bullet did not solve every problem.

He went into the bar and looked around. It was packed with every type of drifter. He had seen so many places like this one: it was the kind of place where the lost scroungers and chancers drifted in, just to have a skinful of whiskey and some company. Someone over in the corner played the piano badly; a line of men at the bar sang or shouted, jabbed each other in the ribs, slapped each other on their backs, and generally acted like old partners, though they were most likely strangers, dried out and bored mindless after too many months out in the border wilderness.

When he reached the only chair and table free from drunks, he sat down, raised a hand while he looked at the bar, where the man standing there knew him and managed a smile; then Jardine called for some attention. A woman was sent over to him. She was young and too thin, like she had been neglected. But she forced a smile. 'Now mister . . . Cal says he knows you and I'm to get you what you want . . . is it a drink or . . . do you want to come upstairs?'

'It's a whiskey I want. A big one. What's your name, Miss?'

She wasn't used to being called 'Miss'. She liked it, and told Jardine so. 'You can call me Miss Liza . . . A whiskey coming up, sir!' She gave a little curtsey, and laughed. 'Most men don't speak polite like that . . . most are lousy rats, like that crowd in the corner . . . see the card players? I dread just walking over there.'

A good woman he thought, though most would call her a whore for doing that work. The world was a cruel place. Surely he was whoring, hiring out his fists and his gun to anyone who would buy him? To hell with the world. It was all wrong, and there was no short answer to all its teasing questions.

Jardine looked across, and he saw four men at the table, with smoke in a grey cloud hanging over them; at first he couldn't make out a face, but then one looked up and glanced around, and there was no mistaking the face of Nunez. Hell, sometimes fate throws in a good hand and offers you a prize, he thought. There is my man, my one true bastard, needing a trip to eternity.

'Miss, would you take my drink to that card table? I'll be over there.'

He stood behind one of the players and stared at Nunez, who put down his hand of cards, tipped his hat up, and sat back, as if he was expecting to use a gun or a knife. 'You! Here you are again, Jardine . . . you cling to me like filthy sweat. I can't wash you off.'

'That's exactly how I feel about you . . . and I got a score to settle.'

'Oh, *señor* . . . a score? Well, I should tell you that these men are with me . . . so you see, four against one . . . the kind of odds a man should run away from, *sí*? So why don't you walk out into the town, take your horse and ride off into nowhere, to some back end of some place where the failures go? You fail in everything, Jardine!'

Just as there was a lull in the hubbub in the bar, Jardine rapped out, 'You don't scare me, you rat.'

The waitress arrived with the whiskey. 'Cal says he don't want no trouble, Mr Jardine.'

Jardine took his drink and knocked it back, then gave her the glass, and she walked away, slowly, edgy.

Too bad the place didn't want no trouble. Nunez could stir up trouble in a mountain stream. Jardine was aiming to put a stop to trouble, large or small, by bringing down the devil who had stalked the land for far too long.

Then the table went over, throwing drinks and

cards over the floor, and sending Nunez and his gang of layabouts sprawling. Jardine threw himself on to Nunez before he could reach for his gun or a knife, and cracked him hard on the jaw. The others now fastened on to Jardine and started hitting him, but they became aware that everybody was standing back and stepping away. Someone grabbed Jardine and hauled him away. Then everybody looked at the line of men before them, and stood still.

There were four men, all wearing long dark jackets, black hats and leather gloves. Three had their rifles pointed at the brawlers; the fourth man was holding Jardine as still as he could, and Jardine had seen the tin stars on all the men in black standing in the line. They were solid, tough. They instilled fear. Then the hard, broad-chested man holding Jardine released him, sensing that not a single man in that corner of the bar was going to move again. The man patted Jardine on the shoulder before he spoke. 'Now, it's the damn Leveller. . . . Joe Jardine. I seen pictures of you, and my deputy here, he's met you afore. Now there's somethin' you gotta register, and you won't like it. First, we don't allow violence in this town. Second, you're looking at three deputies who all fought as Rangers, and whose job it is now to keep the peace. I am Sheriff Bern, and I'm taking you in, Jardine, and you, Mexican bastard, for a night in my jail.'

In no more than a few seconds the deputies had Jardine and Nunez in cuffs and they found themselves being pushed towards the door, with Bern turning around to speak to the drinkers. 'This is a new kind of town. The days of gunfights is done. The days of fightin' over women and cards is done. You all listen close to them words, or you git this.' He held up a tight fist.

Nobody said a word until the lawmen left.

CHAPTER 11

In the hotel, Brett was dressing to go and talk to the people Charlie had gathered for him. There were folk from the Lyceum and from two colleges. There was excitement in town, and everybody was talking about the two Englishmen and their plans. Charlie had been spreading the word all day, and come the evening, there was a crowd of over a hundred citizens in the Lyceum hall.

After Brett went through the initiation of shaking hands with a long line of men in suits and women in long flowery gowns, a gaunt, dignified man approached him and announced rather than merely spoke his name. 'I am Nathan Reiner. I own the Lyceum and take care of the new arrivals in Marshal . . . we're expanding at quite a rate. I am hopeful that you will arouse some interest in this scheme of yours, Sir.'

'I like a touch of optimism, Mr Reiner, thank you.'

'But of course, why go up to Red River county and beyond? Why not stay here?'

'Well, Mr Reiner, you see, I dreamed of a new place, somewhere untouched, open land . . . a place where human society could start again and I could build a world without fear, violence . . . a world where people live together with a common purpose. . . .'

'Well, you describe Marshal when you use those words!'

'Yes, except that it is not *my* town!'

'I suppose you're aiming at being a king in a young kingdom? It smacks of tyranny, to me!' Reiner managed a smile as he said the words, but he still stopped Brett in his tracks, and only when Charlie intervened and led Brett to the platform did the situation ease off.

'Ladies and gentlemen, you have a fine town here. This is surely what the new Texas should look like. There have been wars, battles, heinous violence all around . . . but here you are with a truly civic pride, with colleges and this Lyceum. Well, I am full of admiration for all this, but I am here to offer you another life, one in which everything starts from the first beginning . . . like Eden. In fact, I invite you to join me in making a place called Eden, a place just now beyond any named spot on the maps . . . I believe you simply call it "Indian territory".'

There were gasps. But he was allowed to speak for ten minutes, and then questions were invited. He was told, again, that he was a fool, just as he was told in Bantillo. The questions came hard and fast, and the time wore on. Then someone asked, 'Are you going to invite the Comanche to turn farmers?'

There was laughter – the kind that showed ridicule and satire. Then Brett made ready his answer, the one he had given a hundred times when he had tried to sell his dream:

'The United States was created when folk from my own country wanted a new beginning. They came here with civilized values, wishing to have strangers made into friends, and peace in every corner of their lands. Then your own Texas fought for its freedom from tyranny, and we have this town called Marshal, where travellers come every day, looking for a fresh start in life. . . .'

'My people were the same, mister Brett,' Reiner said, 'They came from Europe, from the old world where a man hates too easily, and where borders and nations scrap like vermin for every scrap of offal. That's why they came here, and that makes me a man with the same aims as you . . . wanting a new life. Difference is, I don't have my head in the clouds!'

'Well, I prefer the clouds to the dog-eat-dog world where the old power reigns.'

The debate went no further. A man came in and whispered in Charlie Gill's ear.

'Seems your guide and gunman has landed up in jail, Brett,' he said.

'See, Brett . . . you're taking the filth with you wherever you go. You hired a criminal!' Reiner said, enjoying his triumph.

Jardine woke early and rubbed his head. It felt as if he had been hit by something rocky. Maybe he had been cracked unconscious by one of these black-coated fools who thought they ran the world? Sheriff Bern was at his desk, and when he saw Jardine stir, he poured him some coffee and took it across.

'Good mornin', Leveller . . . seen your face in the newspapers over the years. Need to thank you for doin' the law's work, though I have to say that I don't approve. I'd say you're a vigilante under another name.'

'I'd say you got a rock for a brain. I just do what you tin stars can't do. That's the truth. Honest folk come to me when you fools ignore them. You just side with the rich folk. I see beyond your black coats and your fancy little ties.'

'Good with words, hey Jardine? Well I have to tell you that words will be no help to you with that attitude. Up there, along the ways, you know what waits for you? You know what waits for all your no-good drifters? The Grim Reaper, my man, the bony man in the long cape. He'll be reapin' you up along with all the other scum like you, and kickin' you to hell.'

Jardine ignored the man, and gave a wry smile in response. He had met the type before. They were all show. They liked dressing up all civilized and clean, but inside they were rotten to the core.

Bern was in his fifties. He had seen all the bad juice that ran through the no-hopers who drifted into his beloved Texas. This man in his cell was no more than one more scrounger leeching on the decent folk. Trouble was, he thought, the man

105

masqueraded as a good man. He was a bundle of lies with a smile.

Jardine was thinking the same about Bern. But any more talk was interrupted by a hand waving out from the bars of the next cell. It was a bare arm, and it had the bell and sabre tattoo visible. Nunez was taunting Jardine, who restrained himself.

'*Buenas dias*, you *gringos* . . . coffee for the real trooper around here?'

'You rat! That's the bell and sabre, so you're with Bria. Well, I'm lookin' for a man who rides with him – a man who's known an Indian scalping knife and survived!'

'Oh really? You want to know a little more about that? Why, that's Juan Bria you're describing . . . the man himself!'

Jardine let the fact settle for a moment. Suddenly, from the man he hated, he had the information he had wanted for years: the identity of Lisa's killer. He knew now that Nunez could lead him to the man.

'Hey, Jardine . . . you ever meet with Bria, he'll show you what a scalpin' is, *sî?*' He gave a nasty laugh, betraying his lack of any morals at all. He was beyond proper human feelings.

Jardine's mind was nagged by the sight of the bell and sabre, and at last the question formed in his mind, 'Hey, Nunez – if you're with Bria, how come he was after your blood that day back on the trail?'

'Ah, poor Jardine . . . you never saw it right did you? Bria wasn't after me. I *led him* to you! Too bad about my partners . . . they had no idea that I was

106

leading them into trouble! But they were not *importante*. You also, tall one, you are worthless – to anybody. What does it feel like to be seen as no more than shit?'

'You shut that ugly face, Nunez!' Bern rapped. 'I only got you two here for the night. You was no more'n a bothersome little snake at a picnic. Mind, I hate to think what you could have done if me and my boys didn't show last night!'

'You know damn well, tin star, what would have happened: I would have run a blade across Jardine's throat.' Nunez forced a laugh at this, though he was the only one who saw any humour.

'Nunez . . . this time you ain't runnin' off . . . your days are numbered. Sheriff, this man knows where I can find the man who killed my wife . . . this man is marked to die real soon.'

'Jardine, I am going to join Bria's army. Think you'll find me then?' Nunez laughed again.

There was no time for an answer, as Brett walked in with Reiner, who stood straight and square before the sheriff and said, 'Morning, Sheriff Bern. I think you'll be releasing Mr Jardine now?'

'Sure, but not the Mexie . . . not yet. I shake 'em both free, there'll be blood up the wall and my jail would shake like a whirlwind hit it.'

'That's right, free the *gringo* and not me! I told you – this is what Texans call the law!'

'Just shut that mouth, Nunez. I'm startin' to find you pesky as the vermin under them floorboards you're standing on!'

The joke worked. Nunez jumped up on to his bed. 'Vermin? You bastard lawman, you think it's amusin', yeah? *You*'re the vermin around here!'

Jardine walked out with Reiner and Brett, back to the hotel. At the door, they stopped, and Brett asked the question that Jardine was expecting: 'Jardine, you coming with us? We leave in two hours. Watt has recovered pretty well, and I got a place in a party heading for Doaksville. I can pay you now, thanks to Mr Reiner. I can pay twenty dollars a day.'

Jardine thought it over. His first thought was that he must wait for Nunez to come out, and then trail him. Yet the money would be useful. He figured that there would be time for both. 'I'll say yes, but I'll meet up with you tomorrow. There's something I must do first.'

'It's a deal. You know the track?'

'Sure. Be with you early tomorrow.'

Jardine went to collect his horse. His instinct told him that if he trailed Nunez, he would be able to nail him before he met up with the Bria fighters. He walked across to the stables and sat, looking over to the jail. He called over the old-timer who had looked after his horse, and took it to the rail where he tethered it while he waited. An hour passed, and he wondered if the sheriff was a man of his word or not. But it was a matter of time, and soon, Nunez would come out of that jail, and he would be ready.

But he saw something else first. From the hotel came Brett, Emily, Duggan and Charlie. Reiner joined them and they shook the older man's hand,

and walked off along the street, where Jardine could see a line of wagons being loaded.

His eyes fixed on Emily, and he thought of her voice, her face, her good strong spirit. He might have lost her, but he could sure take care of her. She was going to need it, once these innocents passed over the Red River and faced their worst nightmare – though naturally, they had no idea what it was that waited for them. But Jardine had, and he knew it was still the same job for him: *hired for hell*, just like always, he said under his breath, so that only his own weather-beaten hide could hear.

But first he had to trail Nunez and settle the score with this Bria. He had no notion of how he could do that. But doubt and confusion had never stopped him levelling where the law had failed, and it wasn't going to stop him now.

CHAPTER 12

As the Brett party's wagons rolled north to Red River county, Jardine waited, and waited. Eventually, out came Nunez, with Bern, who looked around and then pushed the Mexican away, and Jardine saw the man walk towards the stables. It was now a case of stalking him, and the track would lead to Bria.

Jardine had exchanged the mount he had for a tough little bay mare, an animal he knew would last out a long day. He swung into the saddle and plodded along the street, then stopped in shadow until Nunez came out. Sure enough, in just a few minutes, the man was on the road, looking behind him at first, before prodding his heels into his pinto and heading north-west.

The hunt was on. In Jardine's mind there was, over and over, the image of Lisa and her brother, lying there, cut apart by the man with the scalped brow. That man was maybe not too far away now, and Jardine liked that feeling. Yet, as he gradually moved the mare into a gallop, his brain told him that he was as stupid as ever. What was he going to do when he faced Bria? The man had a small army, by all accounts, and he had no answer to that question. He had told himself that he would get even with the Freedom Fighter and Nunez, then head east to meet up with Brett at Doaksville. How simple it all appeared as a thought – but as reality, it was clearly impossible.

He was keeping a long way back behind Nunez, but the Mexican knew he was being followed, of course. Maybe he was misleading Jardine. Maybe there would be a trap? Jardine was tormented with these thoughts and unanswered questions as he rode steadily on, knowing that he was stalking, but maybe being stalked himself.

All the time, with every stride of his mare, Jardine had the picture in his head of what Bria would be like. He imagined that scar on his brow – the long slit where the knife had cut into his flesh, and taken away maybe half of his scalp. It must have been one hell of a painful encounter. It would be rare for a man to survive such a wound, and there would have been a real large flow of blood from him. Now, somewhere up ahead, this man was waiting. Or maybe he was on the move? There was no certainty, but still Jardine had to keep these matters in his head. It fixed his attention on the horizon.

Then, in the late afternoon, the sky made it plain that a storm was coming: Jardine knew all the signs of a severe assault from the heavens. The clouds gathered, and a darkness crept in over the land. It

covered a wide expanse of the territory, and sure as
grass grows on the prairie, it would come down on
Nunez as well. First the clouds seem to press lower.
Then there was a rumble from what sounded like
some kind of mythic creature that had been disturbed and was mad as hell. Then the wind whipped
up.

He managed to move on, with the mare tough
beneath him, facing a wind strong enough to blow
them sideways. But as he came near to some higher
land that would give some cover, Jardine dismounted and led the mare away from the worst of
the storm. It came louder, closer, heavier, and all a
man could do was pull up his collar, keep the horse
close, and wait for it to pass. The rain came like a
great, all-engulfing flood, and he was by a creek –
something he only noticed when he had settled and
turned away from the worst of the weather. He saw
the creek filling up, and the scrub bending.
Mesquite flapped in the wind. Water came down
from the edges of the creek, coming towards him, so
that he had to raise himself a little higher, up into
the track of the storm again, now grasping the
mare's reins and pulling her to him. It would pass,
but it was keeping him penned in. The same, he
thought, would be happening to Nunez. If there was
any way he could go on in this, he could catch
Nunez, but he still had to take the chance that the
main prize was waiting up the track. How he would
face that man was still a problem.

*

The Brett party was now well into Red River country. Brett and Duggan had joined up with a group heading to Doaksville, and they had two long wagons, each with four-horse teams, and then more materials carried on a string of mules. Watt was still not well enough to ride, and he was lying in a wagon, with Emily still nursing him. Brett and Charlie Gill rode in front, both expecting trouble, and Brett repeating his wish that Jardine would show up.

Watt's condition worsened, though he had started off being sure he was fine. But he lost strength, and they soon realized that he still needed rest and sleep, though Brett hoped that the worst of the fever was over. He was worried that his young friend was sinking again; the outlook was far from good – there could be some kind of infection, and there was little in his medicine case to offer a quick cure. When the party stopped for a rest and drinks, coffee was brought to the sick man, and he came round from a long sleep. Emily had been wiping his brow and offering comforting words for hours on end. Now, as they both had coffee, Watt spoke again about what he had said at the hotel. 'Emily . . . I know you said no. I can see that you don't want me . . . not like in marriage . . . but please, please stay with Brett and me . . . come with us up the river. We need a woman. . . .'

'You need a woman? *Any* woman? That sure makes me feel wanted, Watt. No, I'll come with you to Doaksville. Then I'm going to head east to the coast. I don't think the frontier is for me after all.'

113

She thought of the world she had left behind, when its boredom had dragged her down. She thought of all the dinners, the readings, the solemn conversations about the latest sensation, like a Shakespeare production or some serious poetess from the stiff-collar classes in the well-swept streets of the eastern cities, swelling with their pride and self-satisfaction. Now, though, she longed to be back there. The adventure had soured. The one thing she would never forget was meeting Joe Jardine, who had appeared to be the embodiment of the West as she had read about it. She would miss him. Then she was brought roughly back to the present moment by the shaky voice of Watt Duggan.

'What can I do to persuade you?' As he spoke he felt a spasm of pain across his head and dropped his cup. Emily held him as the pain took hold, like a mother with a sick child. The driver up ahead on the seat heard the cry of pain that came from Watt and turned to look behind. 'You coping with him, ma'am?' he asked.

'Sure. He needs Brett to give him something . . . when we reach the river maybe.'

All she could do was offer comfort until Brett took out some more laudanum. Then Watt would sleep again. Her notions of acting and singing, entertaining the folk out in the frontier, were fading fast, and she thought more and more of her life back east. What had her plans of a new beginning brought, she asked herself, apart from the roughneck Lacade and this needy, lost soul of an English countryman adrift

114

in an alien land? No, she would not be his slave in some shack or sod-house. There was no little house-wife inside her.

'Think that Mexie outfit will come at us again, Brett?' Charlie asked, looking around into the distance.

'Who knows? I'm beginning to think that perhaps Jardine was right about me. The visions I had of that new paradise . . . well, they seem like they're evaporating into the air, Mr Gill. Are you still writing up my story?'

'Yep . . . whatever you do out here, it's news. There are other Englishmen out here with crazy ideas, but not on your level . . . not with your particular passions for equality. Most want to take their power with 'em!'

'Thanks. Is that a compliment? I'm not so sure!'

'Without men of vision, Brett, there would have been no journeys west, and no meetings with the peoples who were here long before the travellers from the old lands . . . the people of the buffalo and the endless prairie. It's men like you who opened up minds, recreated all our imaginations. You're a poet somehow, Brett, and I'll write you up that way.'

'Someone from that old world once wrote that great minds are close to madness . . . maybe he was right.'

'I'll pass on that, my friend . . . reserve my judgement!'

Hemmed in by the storm, Jardine turned his mind to thinking about what he had drifted into when he first

115

took Brett's offer. It had been a good way out of reach of the law, but now he found himself tied up in thoughts of vengeance, and he had let the years pass without ever really believing that he would get even for Lisa. Now, stuck out here in nowhere, that vengeance seemed possible, or at least a mite closer. Then there was Emily. He had let her slip away. She had found another, while he, as usual, had allowed the things he really wanted to fade away while he was working to put things right, to apply some real justice. *This is a world without justice,* he thought; *this is some kind of place in the hell the preachers speak about, and I'm stuck in it.*

Then the sky began to clear. He had to gather some strength and some resolve and get moving on again, keeping close to Nunez, who would be soaked like him, maybe no more than a mile away. There was nothing for it but to push on and hope that some clear sky would come along pretty soon. Right now, though the storm was almost over, if he didn't keep going, he could lose the man he tracked. Still he knew, with his body sore and wet but his determination to find Bria still strong, that a dogged pursuit was the only move he could make. He had a vague memory of knowing this stretch of land. He knew most of east Texas, and this place was familiar. The Red River was not so far off, and maybe that was where the Freedom Fighters were waiting, gathering for their next assault on peaceable folk. Though Texas was a fact, and the States were a bigger fact, this bunch refused to say yes to history, and let it just

116

do what it was meant to do. They were standing against change, and there should be some admiration in that – but not when they used bullets, arrows and any other weapons they could muster.

He plodded on, still drenched in a shower, and that was tolerable. Up ahead there was a little more visibility. He stared right in front, and fixed his attention on the track. He saw something moving, way ahead. It seemed to be a number of figures, all swirling around, and there were shouts. Someone was barking out commands.

He quickened the pace a little and the movement came nearer. He made out a rider coming towards him – a lone rider, and he was either waving a rifle, or a hand. It was too blurred to tell. Seconds passed, and Jardine stopped his mare, took out his Walker Colt and waited for the figure to come close enough to be clear. He could only make out the one rider, and all behind that shape in the murk was a sheet of steady rain.

It was Nunez, coming at a gallop. He pulled up real close, dismounted, and ran towards Jardine. 'Don't shoot . . . don't shoot, Jardine . . . we need your help!'

It had to be a trap, Jardine thought. He kept the gun raised and pointed at Nunez's head. But the man held no weapon, and he looked to be in a frenzy, flapping his arms around and then reaching out to stop any gunfire. 'Jardine . . . we need your help. . . .'

'We?'

'*Sí* . . . it's Juan Bria . . . he's gonna die if we don't get your doctor friend! He's gonna die for sure . . . and I can stop these men from killing you . . . if you come with us.'

Jardine was wondering which men Nunez was talking about. Then he was aware of a line of a dozen riders, all coming towards him with the barrels of their rifles pointed at him.

CHAPTER 13

The old-timer was thrown out of the camp, clutching his bag and pulling at the mule he had been given. Juan Bria, from deep inside the pain that was racking his body, shouted for his men to get the man out of his sight. The scene of this explosion of anger was an old shack in the north of Bowie county, where Bria had made his headquarters. The place was hidden away, towered over by a steep incline on one side and a grove of high vegetation on the other.

Bria was no longer young. At fifty, he was still fit enough to lead some of the excursions into Texas to harry and worry anyone who got in his way. But the wounds he had suffered over the years, and the hard life in the open, were taking their toll on him. He lay on a makeshift bed of blankets and straw, while his men fussed and groaned around him, trying to respond to his string of demands and complaints.

He was once stocky, wiry and full of nervy movement, always on the edge of some enterprise. Now, after the last encounter with a party of travellers from

Arkansas heading along the Red River, he had suffered a fall and had had to take to his bed. Some kind of head pain and weakness had followed, and the only man in his outfit who had any claim to medical knowledge was the old-timer. But he was far from adequate for the task.

The leader of the Freedom Fighters had known pain all his life. Nothing had been worse than the fight with the Comanche back in 1855 when he had been closer to death than a lizard's belly to the dirt. He was accustomed to enduring pain. But he sensed that he was in trouble this time, drifting in and out of consciousness.

'You got that no-good charlatan out of my camp?' He screamed at the nearest man. The response was a chorus of '*Sí Commandante, sí. . . .*' from the assembled men who waited for his every order. When Nunez arrived at the camp, and come to Bria to tell him what had been happening in Marshal, Bria soon picked up on the reference to the doctor.

'Look, Nunez . . . you done good. You are one of my best men . . . get me this English doctor . . . bring him here. This is real bad, *amigo*. I have known the agony of having a Comanche knife slide along my brow and damn near finish me, and that was like the torture of devils for weeks . . . but this is almost as bad . . . the hurt is inside . . . it shakes me, makes me sweat like a stream . . . see . . . Go and get this Englishman!'

'If we do that, we could lose valuable time, Commandante . . . you have to come with us. We have to take you to the doctor . . . can you sit in a wagon?'

'Carry me to one . . . get on with it!'

It had happened as soon as Nunez had dismounted and announced his arrival to the camp guards. There had been no time to spare: he was back on the horse and riding with the escort behind him.

He knew that the Brett party were heading out of Marshal, but where? Surely, it had to be the river. Jardine would know, and he was right behind, doing something so wrong-headed that he would be easy prey. They soon found him.

Now they had him leading the way towards the Englishman. Jardine had no choice. They had taken his guns and now he was riding with them, completely at their mercy. But there could be no quick progress. Bria was in the wagon behind, and they could not press on with any real speed.

'Jardine . . . you know who is in this wagon?' Nunez asked, enjoying the torment.

Jardine shook his head.

'In this wagon there is Juan Bria, our leader . . . the Freedom Fighter himself. You are completely defeated by the man who will take Mexico back from the States . . . the last fighter for our great country.'

Nunez had no idea what the power of that information was, how it thumped into Jardine's whole being with the impact of a bullet to the chest. The man he had thought he would never meet, the man who had to pay for what he had done, was a few yards away, in the wagon. Now here he was, the Leveller, unarmed and unable to do anything to that killer behind. He almost laughed with self-mockery, so ridiculous was his situation. There was no other choice though: he had to take the Mexican and his Comancheros to Brett. Otherwise they would just shoot him dead. *Problem is*, he told himself, *they'll kill me as soon as I'm no use to them any more.*

Bria and Nunez had selected twenty men to go with the leader: they were heavily armed, and Jardine knew that they could easily wipe out the Brett party. They would have the element of surprise, and they were mobile and quick; on the other hand, they could not risk any harm coming to Brett himself. That was a restraint on anything they might plan.

Brett and his party were now very close to the river and would soon be over the crossing and moving up to Doaksville. Maybe one day's ride, Charlie told him, would take him from the river up to the town. There he might interest more people in his colony.

Watt was improving. When they stopped to eat, just a few miles from the river, as dusk was thickening, he was well enough to come down from the wagon and sit with the rest, as Brett spoke with his new friends about his Liberocracy.

'You good people . . . you came out here with plans, just as Watt and I did. There's not that much difference between us. For me, I want a new society. Charlie here knows all about it, and he's writing it all up for his newspaper, right, Charlie?'

The newspaper man took out his notebook. 'Sure, I been keeping notes all the way, and there's a wonderful tale to tell, folks. Now I know that you're aimin' to plant yourselves in Doaksville. That makes sense. You got Fort Towson just down the track. I see the sense in that. You're farmers, craftsmen, right? You don't need hi-falutin' notions about a new community. But Brett here has damn near persuaded me, and I'm a hard-headed scribbler!'

Emily was listening, and she had made up her mind about her future. She would head back east from Doaksville, back along to Arkansas and then up through the east back home. She could barely look at Watt, who kept staring at her and then looking away when she saw him. She had turned him down. That hurt a man, she knew that. But it happened every day, to someone, somewhere. She couldn't wait to get transport out of Doaksville and escape the Brett party for good.

Progress was slow for Bria's men. They all knew that they had to get their leader to medical help, but they couldn't rush. They had to keep a steady pace and try to maintain some comfort for the sick man.

For Jardine, he knew that now they were very near the river, and that Brett was maybe only half a day's ride away. When a voice from Bria's wagon shouted that it was time to stop and treat the sick man, he knew it was his last chance to live.

Bria was brought out and he was carried to lie by the firelight when darkness crept in. The shaking of the wagon had been a torment. He felt weak, and wanted to sleep, but he was racked with the throbbing pains in his head, and that ran through his body in spasms.

Nunez, knowing nothing of Jardine's burning desire to rub out every inch of life in Bria, put his prisoner to a wagon-wheel, tied to the spokes. Jardine knew he had to find a way to work himself free. One of the Bria men sat with him, but was anything but vigilant. He was half asleep. He looked around to search for anything that might have a blade or some kind of edge. There was nothing in the dirt; the dozing guard was out of reach. Jardine had been searched and everything taken from his pockets and belt, of course. There was only one thing that had been overlooked, and never before had he been thankful for his little dash of pride in his dress spurs, which he always chose. Even better, the rowels were not ground down, like the OK spurs that were usually treated like that.

The task was now to push off a boot and get to work. The rowels would wear away the ropes if he could push the spurs behind him, towards his hands. It was a tough challenge, but the secret was to work an inch at a time, grasp the spur in his fingers and find a way to rub the rowels on the rope.

With an effort, the right boot was tugged off his foot, and then edged along slowly towards his body. Inch by inch, the spur went closer and closer, until finally he could use his leg no more, and he had to slide his body lower, to allow his fingers to move close enough to take the spur. He looked at the guard, who was still asleep. The talk of the men around thirty feet away was dying down. It would soon be time for them to find a place to sleep.

With one last effort, he touched the rowel edges with his fingers, and shifted the points closer; at first he managed only to move the very edge of the points, and they could not apply pressure to the rope, but then, with a movement of his body one last time, the grip on the rowel was tighter and he began to cut rope.

There were voices saying *buenas noches* not far away, and he could hear moans, most likely from Bria, who was going to find it very hard to sleep. A voice was heard, saying, '*Give him more whiskey . . . more whiskey, Commandante . . . you'll sleep.*' Jardine forced the blade back and forth, pushing hard and fighting off the pain in every muscle of his hand. Then he sensed the ends of frayed rope. Some of the firmness of the rope was rubbed loose. This success gave him one last surge of confidence and he cut with a touch more force. His hands pulled, hoping to drag the rope away from the wheel. At first, nothing gave way, but finally, with one last pull, he lurched free. There was a sound from the wheel, and he thought that the guard had heard. But the man slept on.

Jardine, for a second or so, realized that he was free, and that he was sitting only yards away from Juan Bria, a man he wanted dead. There was an urge in him to forget caution and good sense, and rush to

125

where the man lay, take a knife, and plunge it in his breast. It would be the best value levelling he had ever done. It would be the arm of justice, doing what the law had failed to achieve.

Then the voice of reason took over. He would have to get out of there and find Brett. Emily was there. If he could warn them, find them, take control, then Emily would survive. If Bria's men were to be defeated, then Brett and his friends would need their hired man. He was still that man – the man who had promised to protect them, for only a few dollars, sure, but it wasn't about lucre: it was about honour. Jardine slithered across to the guard and cracked his fist into the man's temple. He went out like a light in a blizzard. Jardine took the man's revolver from his belt.

Now it was a case of finding his mare, which had been tied to the back of the wagon. Jardine moved, bowing low, with the gun cocked ready. There was the mare, with the other horses, tethered and still. With a whisper, he tapped her head and made a low clicking sound, the one she knew. Then he was swinging up and urging her away.

As so often before, he read the sky and headed west to catch sight of the Red River. If he followed that, he would come somewhere close to Brett, as he would head for the crossing south of Doaksville. There were doubts in him; there were worries tugging at him like a child to its mother's gown. But he ignored all the tormenting voices, and when he was clear of the camp, he kicked on, only then remembering that he had left the spur behind. It's a little souvenir for the Mexie bastard he thought, and managed a smile of triumph, that he had escaped a certain ignominious death in the heart of nowhere. Now he had a chance to turn and fight again.

CHAPTER 14

At early dawn the Brett party were packed up and moving north. Watt was well enough to ride now, and Emily sat up front in their wagon, with Charlie at the reins. It was a slow pace, but Brett, riding ahead with Watt, was not worried. The only thing on his mind was Joe Jardine. He would feel more safe and comfortable with the big man riding with him. When he talked about this to Watt, the reply was sharp.

'We don't need the tall man. We have around ten men carrying arms, so if we need to defend ourselves, we can take the assault. Granted, the man saved our necks back there, but we learned, Brett: we learned. In fact we have been learning every single day we've been in this damned land. . . .'

'Damned, you say, Watt? That's not the kind of talk we want. You know, as I do, that we came here to find a blessed land. I'll have no talk of *damned*.'

'I should say cursed then, and we should aim to lift that curse. I say that because we are the new blood here . . . we will change this benighted place into a place of light. . . .'

'Speaking of which, Watt my friend . . . just look at that dawn!'

The first line of orange was spreading slowly across the eastern horizon: it was the early sense of warmth they felt, the moment shortly before the first spike of colour comes and dazzles a man.

'Watt Duggan . . . this is why we came here. This kind of opening up of one's soul is what the poet Wordsworth writes of, do you not think?'

'Poetry is not for me, Brett. You know I'm not a bookish man. Father brought me up to work hay, dig channels, make a tool at the smithy. It was for my elder brother to read books . . . he is now a clergyman.'

'Well now, our Liberocracy shall have a library, you wait and see!'

'Leon, you need a dose of common sense, my friend. Out here the insects chew away at paper I believe. Your books will not last a month!'

There was a shout from behind them. Charlie was calling out Joe Jardine's name. Brett and Watt turned and jogged back.

'Leon . . . look who's here!' Charlie called out. Riding hard alongside the wagon, Joe Jardine was flapping his hat and shouting for them to stop.

'You need to stop and get close up together . . . there's trouble comin' right behind you, Brett!' Jardine said.

'We just packed up . . . only a mile back we were camped.' Watt said.

129

'Sure, but now you're uncamped! Move real quick, and get the other wagons in a line . . . arch around and set close together. Then you all need to find a place under or in a wagon. There's the Comancheros comin' and it's the devil's own son, Nunez, who's leading 'em. Now git shiftin' into positions! But get the women into one wagon and get them out . . . to the crossing and Doaksville . . . right now!'

'But we're almost at the river, Jardine!' Watt was almost raging.

'Sure you are, but *almost* is not good enough. The graveyards are full of fools who said they were almost some place! These are the Freedom Fighters, and Bria, their general, is in a bad way. They're coming for you . . . they'll wipe us out and drag you back to treat their general. You're our best asset here. They can't target you! Now get the women out. . . .'

'That's not very comforting, Jardine. You'll have to improve your skills as a hired gun.'

The other travellers were told of the predicament they were in, and they began to rue the day they had met up with Brett, but there was no time to argue or debate: everyone kept glancing at the horizon, expecting to see riders coming their way, and out for blood. Emily couldn't believe that yet again she was facing danger. Brett ordered her wagon to be the one for the women to take, and the other women and some children joined Emily, ready to move.

Jardine barked out orders, explaining to the strangers who he was. There were grunts and groans as folk did all they could to dig in somewhere and face whatever was coming at them. The day had only just been lit up with that first stab of the sun, and the change from being steady, hopeful travellers to feeling like hunted animals was hitting them all hard. But the fear pushed out any other feelings and filled every one of them with a tense, focused concentration. The only one who kicked against the necessity of setting up a defence was Watt Duggan, who was blaming Jardine.

'Brett,' he told his friend as they both rode a little way out from the wagons to try to pick out movement up ahead, 'the tall man, he's trouble. You took him on when things were desperate. You never advertised. I can see that. But I think you employed not only a man with savagery in him, but a man who attracts trouble like he thrives on it. I've seen men like that before. They bring a dark shadow with them.'

'Well, I can't exactly terminate his employment at this point! Anyway, he might attract trouble, but he does know how to beat it. We have no choice but to let him take control . . . God only knows who or what is going to come across that stretch of plain.'

The wagon with Emily and the women was soon on the move. The travellers were well used to shifting and changing according to conditions, and this was a dire situation. Jardine went to Emily before the wagon pulled out. 'Emily . . . just keep going. This man is coming with you . . . you just head over the Red River and get on to Doaksville . . . don't stop for nothin' . . . you hear?'

131

'I hear.' The man from the immigrant party joined Emily and took the reins. 'They're in your hands, mister,' Jardine said. 'Take good care of Emily Nolan for me.'

He watched the wagon pull out, as a whip snapped with some anger across the team's backs. If nothing else, a stand now, facing Bria's men, would buy some time for the women and children.

Charlie joined Jardine. The expression on his face said everything about the situation. 'Joe . . . you done the right thing. I heard all about this Bria character. He's ruthless, and even worse, he's a man with a special mission from God . . . *his* God, anyways. The word is that he's out to drive every gringo out of Texas and take all the land back for Mexico. My own feeling is that when he was damn-near scalped that time, his brains was took out and he's damned loco. But bein' a newspaperman has some advantages, and one of them is that you hear a lot that is maybe not commonly known. I was told that Bria's men, just a month back, slaughtered two families of German folk coming down towards Lanesport . . . he had children shot, and women were taken away, just like the Comanche do . . . he collects slaves and hostages, Joe. I'm praying that Emily and the other make it over the river.'

'I'm told he has Comanche blood in him, Charlie.' Jardine was checking his stock of slugs, and spinning the chamber of a gun he had borrowed from the man who led the travellers. 'That's not all bad. I mean, those men are never short of courage. The best fighters I ever faced, Charlie. They don't have the kind of beliefs we have about the enemy. No tender feelings in their breasts. But there's no fear there, either.'

'At least we face a mixed bunch ... these are Mexie lancers and swordsmen. Some good shots in there too, at least that was what I gleaned from their attack on us back down there south of Marshal.'

Jardine turned his head and seemed almost to smell at the wind. His face said everything, and Charlie read it like a map. 'They comin' close, Joe?'

'I'd say count to ten and you'll see 'em.'

Jardine shouted out to everyone, 'Now they're mighty close ... check your weapons. Be sure you got plenty of slugs ... wait for my command before you fire at anything.'

Then, before Jardine could say anything else, Brett's voice behind him made all heads turn. The doctor was standing on a heap of smallish rocks. 'Gentlemen, we are eleven standing against what may be a small army ... but I wish to tell you all some-thing vital to our enterprise. I am a man who will now push, lecture, hector any other person ... I am a man who wants to work hard to end violence and killing ... but till I reach the new green pastures, the pure prairie of this land, I have to ask you to take lives. I am no preacher. I have no faith in any God. I consider that man himself will make the changes in the way he lives together. I'm asking you all to recall that when you pull a trigger or throw a knife, you do it so that we can build a world in which knives and guns will not be needed at all, by anyone. Thank you.'

The travellers who had teamed up with him looked puzzled, and not at all impressed. But Watt managed to applaud his old friend, and a few others followed him, not really knowing why.

Then the heads of the defenders turned again, this time facing the east, where a line of riders could now be seen, coming slowly into view. The two wagons left were together, in a wedge shape, and the men were clustered around the wheels; faces looked at faces, hoping for some reassurance that all would turn out well. But the expressions they saw only conveyed anxiety, fear. All they knew was that some Mexies were coming at them.

There were nine men crouched behind the wagons, each one shifting slightly as the riders came nearer; they were trying to find the places with the best view of the enemy. Standing apart from them was first, Charlie, who preferred to be lying flat to the ground, with a rock or two in front to hide his head.

Jardine had a higher place, as he always did when trapped or cornered; he threw together some boxes and packs from the wagons, topped by a saddle, which was fine for resting the stock of his rifle. He had no Colt Dragoon, as that was with Bria now, but he had the Colt Navy revolver he borrowed. His rifle he also took, from the wagon that now carried the women away. This was a .58 Springfield and he was happy enough with it. He could dig in and work pretty quick, at least to the middle distance. He thought it out so that he could do most damage when the Bria horsemen were close up to the wagons.

There were a few shouts from Brett and then from Watt Duggan, who still had his old shotgun, which would spray some lead but would be more effective as a club, Jardine thought with a wry smile.

After a short, nervous silence, they all saw one rider come out of the bunch and head towards them. 'Don't nobody shoot that man!' Jardine shouted.

It was Nunez. He pulled up a few hundred yards away from the wagons and called out, 'Now, we only want the doctor. Just send him out to us, my friends, and we will go. The *Commandante* Juan Bria offers you his word . . . his bond of trust. We want the doctor *hombre* . . . and now. Right now.'

Brett moved towards the horses and peered over their backs. 'I am the doctor, Sir . . . Leon Brett at your service. But unfortunately, my fellow travellers here feel there can be no trust from a man who has in the past tried to wipe us out! I suggest you bring him here, to me.'

Nunez could see, right away, that such a move was a certain way to give the gringos a hostage. Bria might be very sick, but that was not the way to help. He tried to sound patient, but there was some anger seeping through his words now, 'Look, Dr Brett, listen to reason . . . bring your bag of medicines and walk out here . . . you will be returned as soon as my *Generale* is recovered.'

'I can't do that, my friend.' Brett kept the reply short.

'I think I see a man who is not following that oath, right? I am sure you medicos, you have this oath . . . a vow to save lives, no?'

'Not when it risks so many other lives, my friend.'

Nunez was now raging inside, and his effort to remain in control of his language failed. He shouted out: 'Then we will rub you out from life . . . and take you, drag you, to *Commandante* Bria!' His horse reared up and grunted at its rider's impetuous jerk of the reins. Nunez turned around and galloped back to his men.

Brett asked Jardine if he had done well, or made a mistake.

'You did very well, Mr Brett. Now get hold of your gun and find a place to hole up.'

There was another ominous silence – it was one full of a restless fear, and it was a fear they all tried to hold in, as you would try to restrain a spooked mustang. What the wild men out there would do next was not certain, and every handgun and rifle was gripped tight, as sweat ran from every brow behind the wagons.

CHAPTER 15

Jardine had barely any time to think about anything except survival. But now, watching the line of riders facing the wagons, looking like a hawk for the slightest movement, his mind thought of Emily, now heading to the river. She would be moving real slow; but if this fight could delay the Bria Freedom Fighters for a few hours, that might be enough to see Emily and the others safe on the Doaksville track. He thought of Emily, and of the night he lay in her room at the hotel, listening to her breathing. From the time he saved her life, protecting her, she had come into his thoughts.

He had imagined a future with her. It had been in short, vivid images when his mind had found a short while to rest. He had been drifting for years, all the time fighting off his memories of Lisa, because being reminded of what he had lost was too much to bear. He had kept himself on the move, kept looking for work and taking every offer to earn dollars by his fists and his guns – yet now, since that night in the hotel, it was Emily's face that was always coming into his head, offering some kind of hope. But now, he thought of what he had heard on the stairs, and his memory drifted to that scene, when he had heard what Watt Duggan had said.

It was a shout from below that woke him from his reverie. Someone yelled out that the Mexies were coming. He looked up, focusing beyond the wagons, and sure enough, the riders were coming at a gallop. He could make out that some had rifles, and were raising them, ready to fire. A few had bows and arrows. It was plain that there were some Indians, maybe Kiowa he thought, mixed in there. It looked like any kind of mercenary fighter had been drafted into the ranks of Bria's army.

Jardine was high above the action; he could see just about everything. He shouted as loud as he could for everyone to hold their fire. There had to be another few seconds of nervous apprehension before any return of fire. Then some bullets cracked into the wagons, and someone screamed. Jardine knew it was the right moment, and he called out with an effort to be heard above the noise of the pounding hooves, 'Fire!'

There was a volley from Duggan and the others, and two riders fell down, dragged now as their feet stayed in the stirrups. But the others came on, and reached the wagons – there was going to be some close fighting. Brett was still mounted, and standing beneath Jardine; he fired his revolver, picking out a target.

'Brett . . . they can't kill you! They need you . . . get up here!' Jardine called out. Bria's men would have been told to capture Brett, and Nunez knew what the man looked like. It was best to get him hidden from view. Brett scrambled up to join Jardine, who gave him his rifle.

'Now, Brett, stay right here and pick someone to bring down, right? I'm going down there.'

Jardine had seen Nunez, and he marked him out. He slid down a stony slope and then made straight for the Mexican, who had just stuck a knife into a man's chest. Jardine wasted no time, firing at his man, and missing by a whisker. Nunez ran towards Jardine, whose second bullet ripped across a shoulder, leaving the smart of a flesh wound. But the Mexican had his pistol, and his first shot clipped the top of Jardine's left arm. Both were now feeling some real pain, but fought on.

'Nunez . . . time to settle things!' Jardine stood in front of his man, who held a long-bladed knife in one hand and a handgun in the other. 'Jardine . . . *sí*, say your prayers, now!'

He raised his hand and aimed the gun right at Jardine's head, but the tall man thought with the speed of a rattler's spit and went for Nunez's feet. He brought him down to the dust and the gun dropped loose. It was now Jardine's first aim to grasp the man's wrist and get that knife free of his grip. They rolled in the dirt, and the knife was worked free. Then Nunez had the first swing with his fist, hitting Jardine on the side of the head; the tall man reeled back, but before Nunez could retrieve his knife, the force of a blow to the chin knocked him down. He rolled in the dust and tried to pull himself to his feet, but Jardine kicked his head so hard that the Mexican went down again.

As Jardine ran at him, someone else came at him and he had to fight again, as Nunez recovered. The new attacker was a solid, bullish fighter, and he had led with a head-butt. Now Jardine had to wrestle, and he jerked up a knee into the man's face. It was enough to knock him back. Then another punch sent him unconscious.

Jardine had a few seconds to look at what was happening: the riders were trying to get back on their horses and regroup for an attack. But he saw that Nunez was on top of Watt Duggan now, and the Englishman seemed to be wounded. He was clutching one arm. There was no time to delay: Jardine went directly for Nunez, swinging an arm and cracking him hard on the head, so that the man staggered back. He now had another gun and was pointing it at Duggan, who was unable to stand up.

Joe Jardine thought of Emily, this man's future wife. If Watt Duggan died, then Emily Nolan would be damn near being a widow, and that word Jardine hated. He had to move faster than he had ever done before. In a second of sheer determined assault, Jardine had his man by the throat and forced him back. The Mexican's finger squeezed the trigger and a bullet went somewhere high. Jardine pulled his man up and was ready to hit him again, when suddenly

Nunez's whole body went slack and he fell down, dead. Jardine looked up. Brett had seen Nunez, his back to him, and so making an easy target.

The Freedom Fighters were surely going to close in and finish the Brett party, Jardine could see that. It had been a brave stand, but the attackers were going to take the day. Jardine tried to make a head count, but failed, as men were fanned out too wide now. As the Brett party gathered themselves and counted dead and wounded, Duggan, bleeding from a wound in his arm, said, 'Joe Jardine . . . I owe you my life!'

There was then a shock: someone heading the Mexicans called out for a retreat. For some reason, they did not want to finish their enemy.

The settlers were young, and from places way off from where that great battle took place, but they had a vague notion that it was an important word, and they cheered.

'Now, Mr Jardine, Charlie . . . why did they turn away? They could finish us . . . easy!' Brett asked.

'They still need you. You're the doc around here. God knows how many men he's got out there. My guess is that they want someone alive . . . maybe you, Brett.'

Someone called out, 'Hey . . . a rider . . . a single rider!'

Everyone went to the wagons and stared out into the open plain again. There had been no time to check out the dead. Jardine had counted four dead, and Duggan wounded. A second attack would be the

141

end of the Brett party, and himself.

'They could have hundreds back at their main camp,' Charlie said, 'Whether they're all close by, who knows?'

The rider came near and called out, 'Our great *Commandante* says you are noble fighters. He says he would like you in his ranks. But good people, listen. Send out the doctor and we will go. We know brave men when we see them, and your lives will be spared. Send out the doctor and then you all may go north, where you wish.'

'Send out the doctor and we'll never see him again . . . that's a fact!' Charlie said.

'Look, I'll talk to this man. They won't hurt me,' Brett said, then took a few steps out from the wagon, to face the rider.

'Good day, Freedom Fighters. I understand you fight under the sign of the bell and sabre? Well, every regiment has its motto to live by. My own family, the Bretts, have a long pedigree in England, and they have a motto. In English, it's *Hold on to what you have.* Now, I have some friends here, and we have two wagons, some possessions, and plenty of hopes for tomorrow. So you see, I wish to hold on to what I have. Now, if you send one man here, with your general, I will treat him and return him to you, if I *can* help him.'

The rider laughed. 'Oh you Englishman . . . you think I am loco eh? I cannot trust an Englishman! If you have the *Commandante*, you can bargain with us . . . you will have strength. Right now, there are, I think, six of you. Our next attack and . . . the end for you, *señor*. The end. . . .'

'I'll treat him and return him to you. You have my word!' Brett said.

The rider laughed again and swung his horse around, and as he turned he yelled out, 'You die today *señor* . . . you and all your *amigos*.'

Half a mile away, in the back of a cart, Juan Bria was sweating and raging, lying under a blanket, with a man mopping his brow. The Freedom Fighter chief was now begging for help. 'Bring the doctor . . . by heaven, bring him . . . I am going to die here, like a sick dog . . . and it is known that Juan Bria will die in a battle. That was prophesied many years ago! Bring the doctor!'

The riders returned and gave him the unwelcome news. He had to listen as they told him that the doctor would not come, but that he asked for them to bring their chief to him. Bria was desperate. He ranted and snapped out orders. 'For the love of God . . . take me to him!'

But Bria was too sick to look around, and if he had, he would have seen that only a handful of men were with him now, and the hardened fighters around him ignored his command. They had seen their friends shot down by these travellers, and they wanted to wipe out those killers, every last one of them.

The messenger said, '*Generale* . . . they killed Nunez! They are devils . . . savages. They shall die like savages.'

All Bria's men but the one nursing him mounted and rode off, armed and raging, with a desire for vengeance. Bria, even in his fever, knew that he was too far from his main force, and he knew that this last attack had to succeed, or all was lost. '*Companero,*' he said to his friend who was mopping his brow, 'Leave me . . . ride to the men back along in our canyon . . . bring them here . . . go!' It was an old-timer who had stayed with him, and he knew that it was risky to leave his general alone. But Bria managed to gather enough strength to flap an arm at him, as he sat up and pulled a fierce expression.

'Very well . . . I will go. Stay still. Drink as much as you can. I will bring all the men.'

The old man rode off, knowing that if Bria died, he would be blamed. But nobody argued with the general. He dug in his heels and kicked his horse off towards the headquarters of the Freedom Fighters. He had seen sick men before, and he was almost convinced that Bria was beyond help now.

CHAPTER 16

'They'll come again, and this time it's pretty even. We stay in these positions, and we got the advantage.' Charlie was addressing the whole group of desperate defenders. One man spoke his mind to Leon Brett, and was not too happy.

'Mr Brett, we didn't team up with you to find this bunch o' savages after our blood. Who is this general they're talking about?'

'My friend,' Jardine answered, 'This general is a madman who thinks that the war with Mexico never ended. At least, he's taken it on himself to keep the war going. We're caught up in his determined aim to root out anybody who is not a Mexican citizen and send them to hell. I been in wars, and I can tell you that most men who start out sane and respectable in the fightin' . . . well, they come home crazy as a stuck hog.'

The man looked around at his friends, men who had been travelling with him from the Gulf. They were used to Mexicans, but they thought that the time had come for peace everywhere south of the Red River. They were wrong.

'Guess we have no choice, Dr Brett. Unless we ought to trust these man and let you go to tend their boss?'

'I'm quite sure that I would never be seen again back here, or anywhere outside the man's camp,' Brett said.

'Well, we came out here to start afresh, like you and Mr Duggan, so I guess we're together on the main thing . . . keepin' breathin', I reckon . . . that sum it up?' The man said, now managing a slight smile of amusement.

Watt had been on watch and he saw the dirt kicking up. 'Back to your positions, men!' he shouted, and there was a scurrying of men back to their cover. Jardine snapped out orders again, and reminded everyone of the need to hold fire until they heard his command. He went to the spot above them again. This time, there would be far fewer men to deal with in the attack. As the defenders waited in line, the sky lowered again. Jardine thought that there was a string of storms, following the one that had engulfed him; now here was a second wave. There was going to be plenty of rain, right above the plain where they all stood, ready to meet gunfire with gunfire. The sky darkened; there was the beginning of a strong wind, and the rain came at the faces of the men behind the wagons. They could barely see in front of them. Everyone knew that it was going to be impossible to pick targets to shoot at: there was

146

nothing for it but to retreat back towards the edge of rock, behind the ledge where Jardine lay.

Watt and Charlie ushered the others back to whatever cover they could find. Some crouched by low brush; some squatted under ledges of rock. Then there was a terrifying scream and Bria's riders came at the wagons, running around them, and into the neck of the small, tight gulley where the defenders were waiting for them. The riders had no choice but to dismount, and then it was a case of hand-to-hand fighting.

The rain came down in sheets, hitting faces and shoulders like great waves of some restless sea. Every man fighting was gradually coated with water and dirt, and men called out their names so that enemies and allies knew who they were. Some were not keen to pull triggers, and took care to check out who was in front of them before striking out.

Jardine, above, had a better view than most, and he singled out one man from Bria's force, jumping down on him and landing a blow to his face. Then he pounced on top of him and laid him out with a knock-out blow. Everywhere around him there was panic and confusion; the horses hated it too, and their stamping and snorting were heard above the rapping and whipping of the wind into canvas and wood.

It was Brett who came up to Jardine after around twenty minutes of brawling, shouting 'They're on the run . . . look!'

Sure enough, Bria's men were snatching their

mounts and jumping into their saddles, ready to turn away and make for open space. Brett's people had won the day. They all sat around, exhausted, for what seemed to them a stretch of many hours. In fact it was half an hour, but every minute dragged, with the rain and wind still angry and raging. Then gradually, it all died down: the storm had passed, it seemed.

Brett and Watt Duggan looked around, registering faces. Everyone had survived. There were three dead men, though – all Bria's fighters.

'Will they leave us alone now, Jardine?' Watt asked.

'Sure as there's drunks in a saloon! They've had enough. *You* had enough, Englishman?'

Watt Duggan gave Jardine a sour look. He had never liked the gunman, and now it showed more than ever. Jardine was thinking that it was good news that Duggan stood there – good news for Emily. He was so pleased – for Emily's sake – that he said so: 'Well, Duggan, today didn't make a widow anyways!'

The tall Englishman screwed up his brow. 'What did you say, Jardine? A widow?'

'Sure . . . well I guess she's waiting to be your bride, when you get to Doaksville – right?'

'Mr Jardine, you got something very wrong there. She is *not* my betrothed.'

Jardine took this like a punch to the chin. His mind played through the moment on the stairs when he had heard the proposal. Surely there was some mistake. He frowned, gathered some words and said, 'But I heard you . . . I mean you asked her. . . .'

'Jardine, she turned me down! I'm convinced that

she is waiting for someone better . . . she wants a gentleman: something I will never be. Once a ploughboy always a ploughboy. The Norfolk soil clings to me like a curse! It will follow me around the world. I have to say, mind, that she won't want a gunslinger, if that's on your mind!'

Jardine said nothing. He left everyone to make up their own minds about the matter. Deep inside, though, he thought of Emily Nolan, most likely now close to Doaksville, and safe.

'Well, Jardine. You must take me to the sick man – immediately!' Brett said, taking his medicine bag and pulling on the reins of the mare who had served him well on the journey, and who had dodged plenty of bullets. Jardine mounted too, and they set off towards the spot where Bria would be lying, waiting for what he hoped would be a victory against the intruders on his land. 'We'll catch up with you in Doaksville or sooner!' Jardine called out.

The others started cleaning up and making ready to move out. The storm had passed, and now there was only a strong wind, still cutting into their faces, but not powerful enough to sway them as they rode. There ahead was a black dot in the distance, and as they cantered on, the dot became the shape of a wagon. As they came to within a hundred yards of it, Jardine said, 'Now, there could be any bastard there, waiting to put a slug in us . . . in me anyways . . . you're fine till you mend the sick madman . . . let's pray they don't shoot.'

They slowed both horses to a walk. Jardine looked

around, much like a hunted fox would take a careful look at every inch of ground around his one sure safe place. There was no movement except the slapping of canvas on the frame of the wagon. It was a neat, sturdy little cart, pulled by just two horses. They stood still, tethered and free of their harness. One of them snorted, as if he was nervous at something. There was now a little more light, and still that firm breeze.

Just yards away, they both stared at the canvas of the wagon. 'Brett, I'll go take a look, then call for you. You stay right there and keep your rifle cocked. Anything moves, kill it. Even a prairie dog or a snake . . . kill it!'

Jardine walked nervously towards the wagon. He couldn't hear a single sound. Not even the stirring of a man who might be in a fever. One step after another, he inched closer. His handgun was ready to snap out some fire and a lethal slug. Now he was a few steps away from the back of the wagon, and that was open. There had been a cloth over, but it had dropped down and was flapping in the wind.

He was a few yards away from the man who had taken the life of his Lisa. Her face came into his mind again, brighter and clearer than ever before. She was smiling and laughing. There was that light of joy in her eyes. There was the woman he had loved . . . would always love. And inside that wagon was the man who had killed her. Was he sitting there, gun aimed at the back, ready to blast away the face of anybody who appeared before him?

No, it was silent. There wasn't even the sound of breathing as Jardine reached the raised tailboard and then stepped into the space at the back – into a place where anyone inside would clearly see him.

'Bria!' He snapped out, as if he had venom to spit. 'Bria! Time to pay for what you done. Time to pay!'

But no, the man was still. He lay under blankets, just his head showing, and one arm out above a blanket, holding a knife. But he slept. Jardine moved closer. Was he asleep – or was he dead? There was that unmistakable mark of pain across his forehead – the deep scar where the Comanche knife had nearly scalped the man. How had he survived? A voice inside Jardine said, '*He's playing with you . . . he's feigning death.*' Jardine took out his long knife from his belt. He put his gun away in the holster. Then he brought up the tip of the knife blade close to Bria's eyes.

'Reckon it's time somebody finished what the Comanches did that day.'

But no, now Jardine was near enough to sense that there was no breath. There was no life. A closer look made him sure that Juan Bria was no more. Only a corpse lay in those blankets. Jardine put the knife away, and he called for Brett.

'Mother Nature beat me to it,' he said, as Brett came in, with his black bag. 'You won't be needin'' your potions and your pills, Doc. The man's dead as rotten wood.' Jardine left Brett to do whatever is done to dead men. Closed his eyes maybe. Or said a prayer.

There were no prayers for Bria in Jardine's heart. But strangely, he thought, there are no curses either. It was done now, the levelling. The most important levelling of all, this was, and it had been out of his hands. Sometimes a man has to let nature do the killing.

He looked around, and he saw no sign of any of Bria's men. They had run for it, run to save their lives. Maybe they had seen their *Commandante* dead, and let loose to save their skins. Either way, they had left him alone, and he said a prayer for Lisa now, as he sat there, on the dirt, outside that wagon, thinking of nothing at all.

'He's dead all right, Jardine,' Brett said, as he jumped out of the wagon and sat beside the now silent gunman. 'You kill him, Joe?'

'No sir. Reckon he just gave up . . . went over to the land of the shades. He'll find hundreds there who he sent across!'

'A remarkable man . . . he had the worst head wound I ever saw, and I've seen some terrible sights in London morgues!'

Joe Jardine gave his friend a long, searching look. Then he said, 'Brett, you hired a man who had vengeance in his heart. It's not a good thing . . . it's taken me years to learn that fact. Now just you go on to your paradise, and I'll take a while to see if I have a future. You got that? They'll be worried about you.'

'Right. You going to bury this man?'

'I reckon so. Could leave him to the coyotes . . . but. . . .'

They shook hands, and Leon Brett rode back to his wagons. As for Joe Jardine, he looked around and hoped that the Mother Nature who had taken away his enemy might give him some kind of hint about his next move. But there was nothing but that cutting wind and a few restless and hungry horses, and they took no interest in a loner like him, with his mind set on nothing and no future plans except coping with the next minute.

CHAPTER 17

Jardine took some time, and he buried Bria. To do this he had to fight the voice inside, telling him to leave the man out in the air for the vermin. But the sense of decency ran deep in Joe Jardine. It was a shallow grave, and most likely would not keep out the coyotes, but he had done the right thing.

Back where the wagons had camped, there was nobody and nothing. They had all headed out for Doaksville. It was only when Jardine's mind finally came back to consider everyday matters that it dawned on him: he was a wanted man. Sheriff Bern had him down as a killer on the run. But he also thought of Emily Nolan, and where she might be. There was only one choice: did he make for the town and look for her, or did he act like an outlaw and ride west, maybe look for work with the cattlemen?

He decided to get to the river first, and then choose. He rode ahead, steady and slow, and still looking and listening for any trouble. Bria might be dead, but he had an army of followers, and they would not be too far away. They might also be out for vengeance. He quickened his pace and soon reached the Red River. At last, there were people. In fact, there were small crowds there, at a little settlement near the crossing.

Asking around, he found out that Brett and the others had gone across not long before. But Jardine was weary, and there was a bar there, though only a makeshift affair. There was mostly canvas around, but in the midst of these was one solitary shack. The only problem was that around six horses were tethered outside. Looking around, he saw poor folk: there were half-breeds, and there were drunks; a man was trying to sell a mule. A few women were selling something else – their bodies. Yet there was one line of carts and wagons coming along from the east. He needed that drink and some time to rest, but maybe the party coming in needed help. He thought it over, watching the first small wagon pull up, as he stood near the shack. It was then that the reality hit him: the horses in front of him could be Bern's posse.

No, though it was tough, he would stay anonymous, and the next day he would ride to Doaksville. What he hadn't bargained for was Bern himself, walking out of the bar and staring him in the face. There he was, in sombre black, as before, looking more like an undertaker than a lawman.

'Mr Jardine! Good to see you. I been lookin' for you. You know, the law always catches up with a man!'

Jardine's right hand was hanging close to his gun. But Bern had more to say. He smiled. 'Jardine, you see our horses here . . . every saddle the same and every little item we got polished so you see your face in it. Right? Inside this old ruin of a bar I have four deputies, and they all dress the same. They wear black. Same coats, same boots and same hats. You're lookin' at the future, in these men, just as you are in our town of Marshal. It's all built on discipline and rational order. Good name for a new breed of lawmen, you think?'

'This is all very interestin' Sheriff Bern. But I reckon you want me back in your stinkin' jail. So talk straight.'

'Joe Jardine, I've been asking questions about you, and I been hearin' good things about you. You seem to have saved some lives. Seems you're more than a bounty hunter, because I see a man like the Leveller as little more than one of them snakes. Well, I did, afore I come across you, mister.'

'So? When it comes down to it, I'm a hired gun. I do the work that you and your kind will not do.'

'Sure, but there's more to you than that. I been talkin' to Dr Brett, and to Mrs Burke and a host of others. Mr Jardine, I'm gonna tell folks in Marshal that I never saw you, not in no place at all. I'll tell them that you hit out for Arkansas or some place way beyond this trail.'

'You on the level, Bern?'

'You bet. Now I'm goin' back in there, and I don't expect to see you again, anywhere at all. The future of lawmen might be in smart coats and a new rule-book, neat haircuts and polite manners, but there's

156

still a place to apply something that shifts a mite. Now shake my hand.'

They shook hands, with the lawman still smiling. The he said, 'You're a good man, Jardine. I wish you well.' He turned away and joined his men inside.

Jardine felt a sense of relief wash over him. The last thing he had wanted was another fight. The trail to the Red River had wrung out of him every last drop of his strength, and he was still looking at the horizon to the west. It was Indian Territory. It was wild. But there would always be fools like Brett and Duggan who would go there with an innocence that would spell their ruin. They would need Jardines, he thought.

Now, before he headed out into nowhere in particular, Joe Jardine had one more thing to do. He rode into Doaksville and asked around about a pretty little actress, an entertainer called Emily Nolan. Man after man shook his head. But finally, he reached the newspaper office, and there, drinking whiskey with a man at a desk, was Charlie Gill. Charlie and Joe were glad to meet up again, and Charlie had plenty of news.

'They left yesterday, Brett and company . . . still bent on that Liberocracy, and still headin' up to the Kimishi. Never seen a man so eager to lose his scalp! But he will not listen to reason, and the tall one, Duggan, went with him. Looks like that Caldy character did get back and made somethin' happen, Joe. To be honest, we never thought we would see you again, after Brett told us about you stayin' with the

Mexican. We expected his hundreds of savages to cut you into little pieces. But I should have known that Joe Jardine would come out of a scrap and fight again!'

'I sure am sick of fightin' right now, Charlie. Sittin' at a desk looks mighty fine as a way of life, from where I'm lookin', that is.'

The man at the desk was the editor of the local paper, and he had already been told of Jardine's exploits along the trail from Bantillo. 'Been told all about you, mister . . . you're gonna be in my news-sheets. You like the notion of a little notoriety?'

'Not at all. Please don't sweeten it up into some kind of drama!'

Charlie changed the subject. He knew too well what was on his friend's mind. 'I know what you want to ask me, Joe . . . ask away,' he said.

'Emily Nolan?' Jardine asked. Charlie was reading his friend's mind. It was all there in his face – his affection for the woman.

'Have one more whiskey and then head for the New Empire . . . it's in the better part of town, where folks use cutlery and say *Pardon me, Sir.* . . .' Charlie laughed. 'Now, Joe my friend, I have some cash for you. Dr Brett told me he sold some things so he could pay you. He told me you saved him and his people from a certain death out there.' He handed over a roll of dollars. 'I just hope he does well out beyond the forts and the Rangers. The new troops from the government seem to spend their time drilling inside the stockades! I'm writing a piece on that right now, to try to stir things up at West Point or in Washington!'

'Good luck, Charlie,' he said, and the friends parted with good wishes.

'Go to the Empire and see her, Joe . . . she's so fine!' Charlie said.

Jardine arrived there at dusk, after seeing to some business. It was a grand place, the Empire. It stood apart, with land all around it, and small trees in line. There were buggies in a row, and then stables, where the ostlers wore some kind of livery. It could have been a little version of Paris, he thought, like he had seen in the periodicals.

There was piano music playing, and then applause, as he walked in and paid for a seat. He sat at the back, trying to understand what exactly was in his mind. He saw glimpses of himself, sitting across for her at a dinner table; he saw candles and wine. She would look at him showing the warmth in her heart. . . .

There she was, at the piano, and she now stood up, told a story of old Europe and what it was like in Vienna. Then she sat and made ready to play again. She wore a pretty yellow dress and her hair was in rich, shiny curls. She let her gaze scan the whole theatre now, and Jardine thought what a panic he would feel if she could see him there. Then she said, 'This is a piece by Joseph Haydn.' Emily was beautiful, Jardine thought, like an angel. Somewhere there would be a man who could tolerate itchy suits and talk about piano quartets. That man, he thought, does not sit easy inside me, though I wish her such happiness.

Jardine now had some cash in his pocket. A night's rest was just what he needed, and for once, it was a peaceful night, with no visions of the painful past. All he could do was imagine what lay a hundred miles off, or a few days' ride into an open space. There was a feeling welling up in him that he had not sensed for some time: that joyful lift of the spirit a man has when the immensity of the plains expands before his eyes, or at least in his mind. That was happening to him now.

At sun-up he hit out for somewhere west, equipped now to set out afresh, with a new little sturdy mare who would gallop most of the day, and some new leather for the guns and the hardtack. He had made a tough decision, and thought long and hard, but in the end, there was something out there, way beyond the trail from the north east where the new settlers were rolling in.

What that something was stayed a mystery. Yet it was calling for him, and he had no argument against it.